I0556242

SECOND BLOOD
A Reverse Harem Tale

Lovin' the Coven, book 2

by

Jacquelyn Faye

SECOND BLOOD
A Reverse Harem Tale

Lovin' the Coven, book 2

All Rights Reserved
Copyright © 2019 by Jacquelyn Faye
Cover Design © 2019 by Sean Hayden
Cover Photo © 2019 by Depositphotos/inarik
Cover Photo © 2019 by Depositphotos/debramillet
Cover Photo © 2019 by Depositphotos/xixinxing

ISBN: 978-1-945893-08-7

Published by Untold Press LLC
114 NE Estia Lane
Port St Lucie, FL 34983

www.untoldpress.com

PRODUCED IN THE UNITED STATES OF AMERICA

10 9 8 7 6 5 4 3 2 1

Dedication

To the broken, the beaten, and the damned

Keep marching

CHAPTER 1

It never ceases to amaze me how even when you're immortal life just keeps on chugging along too fast to believe. In the short span of a couple of weeks I'd manage to move to another city four states away from my beloved Virginia, join and become high priestess of a new coven, get blown up, buy a house and a fire house, solve a murder, and pick up two boyfriends at the same time…

While life passes quickly, *nobody* ever said it was easy.

Leaving my mother's house, a home I had lived in for ninety-nine years, hadn't been the easiest life decision I'd ever made. In my defense, I was driven by the goddess and had little choice in the matter. Judging from how my mother reacted, you'd never have been able to guess that, though. She took it as a personal affront.

Josie, my best friend and another witch, made the move with me. When we left, I had nothing more than a general direction of where I needed to go. We ended up in Cedar Falls, New York. A town a lot quainter than Ashville and in desperate financial status. We also happened across the local coven, which the chief of police and several of the local fire department happened to be a part of. That's when the murders started happening. We managed to figure out who the killer was, but not before we lost several people who would be sorely missed.

The doorbell ringing during our celebratory dinner had been odd. I should have followed my gut something wasn't quite right. As it was, here I stood with a vampire in front of me asking for the coven's help.

My hand reflexively covered my bald head, my hair had been totally singed off in a fiery car wreck. It was epic, but I should have grown my hair back sooner. The guys had been begging me, but I kind of enjoyed teasing them with it.

The vampire was staring at me shyly, grateful to be out of the cold. I just couldn't believe I had invited him in my house so willingly. In my defense, I hadn't known he was a vampire, but still…

"I'm sorry, what?"

"We need your help. I was informed that you were a coven of witches for hire?"

Ahhh. That explains it…

"Formerly for hire… We, sadly, are not what we once were."

"The Coven of the Gold Moon is legendary for their magic…"

"Which is probably why we're now the Coven of the First Moon."

His face fell. "I am sorry to have bothered you."

"Wait." Lady damn it all, I could at least hear him out. "I didn't say we wouldn't help. I'm just letting you know we might not be able to."

He turned and stared at me in confusion.

"Look. Let's start over. Hi. I'm Dot." I reached out and offered him my hand. Vampire or not, I could still be polite.

He removed his glove and held out his pale white hand, gingerly encircling mine and smiling. "And I am Amir."

"Would you care to sit?" I motioned at the couch behind him. The dining room was heavily occupied, as was the kitchen. The noise levels almost drowning out our conversation.

"I can come back…"

"It's okay. Are you hungry?" I realized I probably should *not* have asked that as soon as the words slipped from my mouth. I wasn't sure if vampires could eat human food, and I sure the hell wasn't offering him a vein. I didn't care *how* unnaturally beautiful he was. "Can you eat Italian food? I know there's a ton of garlic."

He chuckled and removed his coat. It had hung down to his knees, so I didn't notice the leather pants he wore until I saw them tucked into matching boots. They were…tight. Very tight. "I can not partake in actual food, but I appreciate the offer."

"What about drinks?"

He paused and his cheeks rose a little as a partial smile crossed his face. "Do you have any wine?"

"Red?"

"Of course…"

I took his jacket, hanging it on the rack by the door, and headed for the kitchen. "I'll be right back," I called over my shoulder.

Chief was standing at the back of the line, watching the scenario as it played out. I gave him my best *I need you but not in a sexual way right now* look.

He dislodged himself from the food line and met me in the kitchen.

"All okay?"

"Oh, yeah, sure. Just invited a vampire into my house. He wanted to hire the coven to help save his clan. Now I'm getting him a glass of wine. The usual."

"Excuse me?"

"You heard me. Want to be my backup?"

"Always."

"Grab a drink."

I poured him a glass of red wine, right out of the box, grabbed the one I had left on the counter, and waited for Chief. He popped a cap off a fresh bottle of beer and followed me back into the living room.

I handed Amir the glass of wine and sat down on the love seat. Chief plopped down next to me, taking a swig from his beer. "Amir, this is the chief of police, and a member of our coven, Bill. Bill, this is Amir. He's asked for our help." I sounded stupid, even to myself. I didn't do well in uncomfortable situations and I couldn't imagine the night getting anymore awkward.

Bill reached across the table and shook his hand. "Excuse our high priestess. She's socially inept."

I was wrong. It did get more awkward.

Amir laughed, his otherworldly voice sending chills up my arms and down my spine. "What was that?"

"My apologies. Our voices…they are meant to entrance humans."

"What about witches?"

He shrugged. "You are the first I have met."

"Why don't you tell us what's going on?" Bill tried to get to the point.

I nodded.

The vampire sighed, sipping his wine and leaning forward to set it on the table next to the empty bottle chief had put down. He placed his elbows on his knees and stayed where he was, pressing his hands together. "Our clan lives north of here in a small village. We do what we can to survive and not draw attention to ourselves, but that is no longer the case. Over the past few weeks… Excuse me, I do not know where to start." He reached down and picked up his wine, tasting it and letting it roll around his tongue before swallowing it slowly. I could see him gathering his thoughts.

"Take your time," I said quietly and waited. Chief's hand touched my back and begin to rub me affectionately as he sat back in the love seat.

"It started three weeks ago. We were in the wilderness on a hunt… Three of us. We heard what sounded like thunder and Janus screeched, the sound scattering the wildlife around us. When we emerged from our cloaking camouflage, Janus was gone. Yvette and I assumed he had gone back to our village, but when we returned, he was not there. The next evening, we searched and searched, but found no trace of him. It was as if he vanished into the air."

"What were you hunting?" I tried to sound curious, but it came out accusing, even to my ears. Chief nudged me in the back. "I didn't mean that the way it sounded."

Amir chortled. "Yes, you did. It is okay, though. I understand. The truth is we were hunting bear. It has become too dangerous to hunt humans in the past century. We have had to adjust our diet."

That didn't make me feel any better. "Do you think he was attacked by a bear?"

"No. There would have been signs of a struggle. And the chances of a bear winning against a child of the night…"

"Sorry to interrupt. Continue with your tale?"

He nodded, taking another sip of wine. "Two days later we found him."

"Alive?"

"No. He was chained to a stone altar in the woods. Drained of his blood."

"Somebody drank his blood until he died?"

Amir shrugged. "There is more. He was drained of his blood and most, if not all, of his organs were missing."

"So, it wasn't another vampire."

"No. We cannot feed from each other. It is poison to us."

"I'm guessing he wasn't the only one?"

"No. Since then, two more of us have been found the same way, drained and robbed of our organs."

I looked over at Chief. "Any thoughts?"

"The same ones you probably are having right now."

"You know something?" Amir sounded hopeful.

"Yeah, but it's probably nothing you would want to hear."

He shook his head sadly. "At this point, the bitter truth would be welcome over blind ignorance."

"Sounds like you are being hunted by witches. Vampire blood, fae blood, werewolf blood… These are all very powerful things. Many witches who have left the Lady's graces often seek power through such things. I am sorry."

He backed up a little, fear plainly etched across his face. "You?"

I held up my hands. "No. We do not trade in death. You are safe. I was apologizing for what has happened. How many are in your clan?"

"There are eight of us left."

"Where is your village?"

"Just over the border into Canada."

"Eight of you for an entire village?"

He sighed. "We used to number more in times past, but this world is changing rapidly. We are the stuff of legends, as I'm sure you are familiar. We do not fit in anymore. We were hunted almost to the point of extinction by humans. Those of us who did not want to go off into the cold night, became hermits and banded together. We live in caves and huts, far away from the prying eyes of the humans around us, giving them no reason to think we are real."

"Not all of you."

"Pardon?"

The thought of them living so primitively, broke my heart.. There were a clan of vampires back home who had sought protection and became prosperous, healthy, well adjusted, and liked by the community. Their Halloween decorations usually won the annual competition, much to the chagrin of my mother.

"What if I told you that you didn't need to live like this?"

"I do not see how things can be different."

"Can you be trusted around humans?"

He looked at Bill like I had lost my mind. I turned to get his reaction. It mirrored Amir's. This wasn't going to be as easy as I thought.

"Amir. I'm from a town on the east coast. The witch population is over seventy. There is also a family of lycanthropes who live there. As well as a…clan of vampires. They run the blood bank and are valued members of the community. We have fae visitors as well. What is truly unique about Ashville is the supernatural community lives in harmony with the human population."

"How?"

"Centuries of prosperity. This town is far from that, but it is my goal to accomplish much the same, and we are off to a rocky, but good, start. Would you be interested in moving here where it's safe?"

"I am the chief of our clan, but I can not speak for all in this. This is…too much?"

His French accent became a little more prevalent. "Would you consider it if they agreed? I would help you transition if I thought you could be trusted."

"What is a blood bank?"

"Human's donate blood and it is kept frozen. It's used to treat humans in hospitals who suffer traumatic injuries and require transfusions. The vampires supply this donated blood and live off the excess."

He stared at me in horror.

I sighed, at a loss how to explain it better. I looked at Bill and couldn't read the look he was giving me. I'd talk to him later.

"This. I… Would you excuse me? I need to ponder your words. Would it be alright for me to return in two days time?"

"Sure. Take all the time you need."

He stood and bowed. "I thank you for your hospitality." He headed for the front door, retrieving his jacket and practically running out of the house.

At least I had given him an option. I sighed and turned to Bill.

"Are you fucking insane?"

That's when I noticed the coven standing in the entrance to the living room, listening to the entire conversation. Some held plates of food in their hands, still eating and watching the entertainment.

"What?"

"I asked you if you had finally flipped your lid. How could you invite an entire coven of blood-sucking vampires to relocate to our town?"

"They need help."

"So do you, Dot."

Bill got up from the couch, grabbed his empty beer and walked away, leaving me sitting there in shock from his unexpected anger. "What did you want me to do?"

"Hear him out. Kick him out. Get on with our lives?" He grabbed a plate off the counter after parting the sea of gawkers.

"You would just leave them to be slaughtered by rogue witches making potions they shouldn't be?"

"They're vampires, Dot. They can fend for themselves. Hell, one of them could probably wipe out the whole town. You want eight of them running around Cedar Falls? Really? That was your plan?"

I chugged my wine and walked over, grabbing a plate and taking some chicken and pasta. I didn't feel like having any of the garlic bread. I loved the stuff but hated having the aftertaste in my mouth for the rest of the night.

He took a seat at the dining room table. I finished shoveling food on my plate and took the seat next to him at the head of the table. "We are in a unique position to help them, just as they could possibly help us in the future. When I'm telling you the vampires in Ashville integrated just fine, I mean it. Do you know what the crime rate is in town?"

"Are we counting your mother in this rate or just petty crimes?" My brows rose at his snarky tone as he shoveled a forkful of twisted spaghetti into his mouth. He was *really* angry.

"Zero, Chief Dick. There hasn't been a murder in Ashville in thirty years."

"This isn't Ashville, Lady Asshat."

I regretted my decision not to grab a piece of garlic bread. It would have complemented the acidity of the sauce perfectly. I looked over at the trays. Candace was standing there nibbling on un-sauced noodles. "Candace, could you toss me a piece of bread, please?" I turned back to Bill. "Listen, Mr. Douchenugget. I'm telling you we can have what they have. You just need to trust me a little bit."

"Before or after the population is sucked dry? Should we wander around the forest and find some werebears? The humans can run around with porkchops tied to their waists and they can all play tag! This food is really good. Is there any more wine?"

Candace handed me a slab of bread and someone else set the box of wine and a glass down in front of us. I sloshed some in the glass and slammed it down in front of him. "Let's not be fucking ridiculous! I'm talking about helping a small coven of vampires who have been reduced to living like cave people. How fair is that?"

"Fairer than letting the people get turned into juice pouches!" He took a sip of wine. "Ooh. That's good, too. Beer just doesn't go with Italian."

"I thought you drank beer with everything. Juice pouches was a good one, though. But come on! Do you think I would put the people of this town at risk? Why would I? If I couldn't handle the situation, I wouldn't have fucking suggested it."

"Could you pass the salt? And why the fuck would I think you could handle it? Since you've been here, you've been blown up *twice*, almost got shot, and almost got three people of the coven killed? You don't even have any fucking hair, *Dot.*"

I rubbed my head absentmindedly. He did have a point. "Yeah, well, you're a dick!"

I pushed my food away, stood, and stopped.

The coven was standing in a semi-circle around the table. They looked like kids watching Mom and Dad fighting about whose turn it was to empty the dishwasher. I sat back down and let out the breath I'd sucked in, staring hopelessly at Jimmy. He gave me a small smile, but didn't look too thrilled with me, either.

CHAPTER 2

Picturing the chief's face, I crumpled up the last of the foil pans and stuffed it in the nearly full bag of trash I had pulled out of the garbage can. "Asshat."

"He's kind of right, you know."

"Don't start with me, Josie."

It was official. They were ganging up on me.

She sighed, sitting at the kitchen counter with Candace. Everyone else had left after the fireworks between Chief and I ended. "You know you screwed up. It's why you're being bitchy and carrying on."

"I know. But they don't know that."

"Looked like Chief figured it out."

"I don't understand?" Candace sounded confused.

"Dot should have talked to us before offering the vampires sanctuary. She knows she screwed up, so she's being an asshole to everybody."

"But she is the Lady? Our opinions do not matter."

"Oh, sweetie. Maybe in some places, but not here." She leaned over and kissed Candace on the head.

At least Candace was on my side. "I… Okay. Yes. I fucked up. I'm sorry."

"I'm not the one you should be apologizing to."

"Well, he can wait."

The doorbell chimed merrily. I wanted to rip it off the wall and stuff it in the garbage disposal. "Could one of you get that? If it's Chief, slam the door in his face, please."

Candace got up and headed toward the door.

"I wasn't talking about him."

"Who then?"

"The entire coven. You didn't consult anybody."

"So, I was supposed to hold a town meeting while the vampire was asking for help?"

"No, but you should have told him you needed to discuss it with your coven and asked him to come back."

I sighed. I hated it when Josie was right. I really did.

The door slammed shut and Candace came back in and plopped down next to Josie. I stared at her expectantly and then looked toward the living room. "Who was it?"

"Chief."

I laughed. "Let me guess. You slammed the door in his face."

She blinked. "Was I not supposed to?"

I smiled and shook my head. Josie gave her a hug and I headed toward the front door. I opened it just as a very confused looking Chief was about to knock on it. "Come in."

I turned around, and headed back to the kitchen, leaving the door open for him this time.

I opened the door of the non-working fridge and stuck my empty glass of wine under the nearly empty box of wine, twisting the spigot.

"May I have a glass?"

"There's beer left if you'd rather."

"Wine is fine. I still have the taste of garlic bread in my mouth."

I grabbed a water glass out of the cupboard and filled it for him. All the wine glasses were in the dishwasher. Thankfully, it was the one appliance still working. My new set would be here tomorrow, and I couldn't be happier. "Out of wine glasses."

"This is fine."

"Come on, Candace. Let's let the big people talk." Josie grabbed her hand and they headed for Josie's room.

Chief sighed. "Dot–"

"I'm sorry." I didn't give him the chance to finish.

"What?"

"I'm not saying it again. You heard me."

"I seriously didn't hear what you said."

"I…am…sorry," I reiterated slowly.

"I know. I heard you."

"Did you seriously come here to fight?"

"No. I came here to apologize."

"Wait, what?"

"I…am…sorry…too."

"We're a mess. Want to sit and talk somewhere a little more comfortable?"

"Sure."

I took my glass of wine and headed toward the living room. I parked my butt on the love seat and pointed at the couch. Not that I didn't want to sit next to him, I just wanted to face him while we talked.

"Well, I apologized for being a bitch and not consulting everyone first. What are you sorry for?"

"For not talking to you about it after and starting the fight because I was angry."

"I do have that effect on you."

"You do. But what I did was inexcusable. You *are* the high priestess and they came to the coven. I was angry as the chief of police whose job it is to keep the town safe."

I drank some more wine, thinking about things from his point of view. "Back home…and I know you're probably sick of me saying that, and I'm sorry…my mother is the high priestess of the largest coven outside of Europe. My grandmother basically carved the town out of the wilderness and ruled over it. My mother became high priestess and reigned through the invention of the telephone, automobiles, and iPads. She's had to deal with losing part of her authority to human figureheads and law enforcement, but now they work together harmoniously. Well, maybe not the mayor, but that's because he made fun of my mother's brownies at one of the fundraisers."

"That's what started the horse's ass feud?"

"Yeah… Did I mention my mother is quite petty?"

"Didn't need to."

"She doesn't hide it." I snorted.

He slid forward in the seat. "So, how does she make it work with the chief of police, there?"

"She's been boinking him for forty-something years. He's in his seventies now and she still enjoys it. He gets off, she gets what she wants."

"Is that what you are suggesting we do in this situation?"

"No. In fact, the odds of me having sex with you went down exponentially earlier this evening."

He winced.

"*Until* you apologized as well. I was being an uppity shit, you called me on it, and still apologized."

"So…"

"We both were wrong for different reasons. We need to discuss this and come up with a solution."

"Agreed."

I lifted my glass in a toast.

"To a *long* and prosperous working relationship."

"Was that a penis reference?" I snickered.

"What? No!"

"Cuz it sounded like one."

"Dot, I swear!"

"You're not allowed to use the word long anymore. Ever." I couldn't help it. I was teasing him, and he was squirming. It was delightful.

"You're fucking with me right now, aren't you?"

I smiled at him over the rim of my glass. "Maybe."

He gulped his glass of wine and grabbed mine as he passed me on the way to the kitchen. "Is this stuff any better cold?"

"Worse. Box wine should never be cold, I think it turns into kerosene."

"That might taste better."

"There's a bottle of good shit in the cabinet above the fridge. Want me to open it?"

"I got it."

I heard the cabinet open and the bottle slide out. He came back into the living room and sat down next to me, whispering, "*Yn agored.*"

The cork burst through the foil cover and he caught it with his empty hand. He sniffed the open bottle, winced, and took a long swig, passing it to me.

"Classy," I said and did the same. The difference between the bottle and box was moonshine and kerosene. They'd both fuck you up, but one might kill you.

I turned and put my back against the arm of the loveseat, sliding my legs over his and getting comfortable. I took another swig and handed it to him.

"So, what do you think we should do?"

He turned, looked at me, and snickered. "Could you please grow your hair back? I mean really. It's getting hard to have a conversation with you. I couldn't even look at you when we were fighting. I would have given up if I could."

"*Ag fás,*" I said, picturing my shoulder length, red hair. I could feel it growing and wanted to scream and scratch my head. Not the most pleasant feeling in the world. "Better?"

"Horribly uncomfortable to watch, but yes."

"My mother used that spell on the mayor's back at a picnic one year."

"That's mean."

"Did you just meet my mother?"

"Technically, yes."

I rolled my eyes and grabbed the bottle from him. A long pull later and I handed it back. "At least we never saw him in a tank top again."

The chief grinned. "So. Vampires. Do you *honestly* think they can come here and live among the humans?"

"*Honestly*, I think they can. Is there a blood bank in town?"

"Yes. Believe it or not, we supply a lot of the blood to the surrounding cities."

"How?"

"People are broke. They sell their plasma and platelets for cash. I think they even give away movie tickets for regular blood donations. The theater here closed, but the one in Amersville is open."

"That's sad. Is it for sale?"

"What?"

"The blood bank?"

"How the hell would I know?"

"Well, it would be easier than dealing with competition."

"You *are* insane."

"Did you just meet me?"

"Technically, yes."

"Oh, stop. You've known me for like two weeks now," I said and snagged the bottle. Or tried to. Chief took another swing before letting me have it. I tipped it back and poured the tiny bit into my mouth that was left. "Was there another one up there?"

"Yeah. Like three people brought you wine as a house warming gift. Should I grab another?"

"Unless you feel like drinking out of the box."

"I'll grab another. I'm not that brave." He lifted my legs, sliding out from under them.

"I know."

"What's that supposed to mean?" He called from the kitchen.

"Oh, I don't know."

He used his spell to pop the cork and set it on the kitchen counter as he walked back into the living room "Because I'm leery about having a clan of vampires move into town?"

22

"No. That was a snide remark about you being a chicken."

"I'm a chicken?"

"Yep. Cluck cluck."

"Wow. You're drunk."

"So're you."

He drank and handed the bottle to me. "Yeah, but I'm a sweet drunk. You're kinda mean with your chicken noises 'n shit."

"Cluck cluck."

"So, why exactly am I a chicken?"

"Cuz you wouldn't get into the shower with me. Had to wash myself all by my lonesome." I took a couple of gulps and pointed the bottle at him. "Chicken."

"That's hardly fair. I wasn't the only one you invited."

"So? My shower is plenty big."

"I'm not showering with another guy."

"Haven't you ever been in a locker room?"

"Yes."

"Have you ever seen a grown man naked, Joey?"

"What?"

"Have you ever seen a gladiator movie, Joey?"

"You *are* drunk."

"Maybies." I took another drink. "Have you ever been in a Turkish Prison?"

"Give me that." He snagged it from me and downed the rest of it.

"Wow. That was mean." I scooted my butt closer to him and put my legs back over his. His hand slowly crept up my leg and settled on my knee.

"So was asking me to shower with Jimmy. I like the guy, but not that much."

"It's not like I was going to fuck you both in the shower. I just thought it would be fun."

His hand started making lazy circles on my knee. I was wearing leggings. It kind of made me wish I had worn a dress. I was concentrating very hard on what that would have felt like on bare skin.

"Woah. Now I'm drunk." He started laughing.

"Good. You're more fun when you're drunk."

"I know. I'm boring."

"Ha! No, you're not. You're just more playful."

"How?"

"You touch me more."

"You like to be touched?"

"Sometimes," I said and smiled seductively. But, then again, I was pretty shitfaced. I might have been grinning at him like a roofied caribou.

"You're sexier when you drink, so I touch you more." To illustrate his point, he slid his hand from my knee up over my lower abdomen and down my other leg.

"That tingles. So, I'm not sexy when I'm not drunk? Is that what you are saying?"

"Not at all. You are incredibly sexy when you're sober, you just become even *sexier* when you drink, and I can no longer resist your sexy seductive temptations."

"So, I'm sexy *and* seductive when I drink. Gotcha." I spread my legs open and struck a pose. I have no idea what pose I struck, but he started laughing. However, his hand did come to rest on my inner thigh, so I did something right.

My thoughts drifted to the shower again. "You should have sucked it up and had that shower with me."

"I don't see you yelling at Jimmy for not agreeing, either."

"He's not here."

"No. He's not." For all his noble words about not getting jealous, he sure sounded it.

"Are you jealous?"

"Me? No. Not even a little."

"Cuz you shouldn't be."

"Good, cuz I'm not."

"Kinda sound it."

"Nope."

"Okay. I'm just sayin'."

He gripped my thigh in his hand. "Do I?"

"What are you doing?"

"Do I sound jealous?"

He squeezed my leg a little. It sent a jolting spasm through my leg, causing me to arch my back and lift my butt off the couch. "No!" I gave him a dirty look when he stopped.

"Am I jealous?" He gave me an innocent smile.

"Maybe." He squeezed again and I howled like a banshee as I twisted in my seat, trying to free my leg from his grip. Then he let go again.

"Am I jealous?"

"No, you bastard. You're not jealous."

"See. I told you."

CHAPTER 3

A light, rhythmic tapping on my forehead woke me from my zinfandel induced slumber. My eyes opened and crossed, focusing on the feminine finger raising and plunging on the spot between my eyebrows.

"Don't make me magick your armpit hair into steel wool."

The finger disappeared and was replaced with a very amused looking Josie face. I groaned and rolled over, my hips bending at an uncomfortable angle as the chief was still under me.

"I don't have any armpit hair."

"I'll grow you some," I said and closed my eyes, wiggling my butt and trying to get comfortable.

"No make-up sex?"

"No. One of us passed out. Not sure who though."

"Yeah. I think you both did."

"What is that fucking noise?" I sat up, looking around and sighing when I realized it was him, snoring beside me. "Lady, he sounds like a friggin' chainsaw."

"And you sounded like a woodchipper until I woke you up."

"I don't snore. Shut your face hole."

"Are you *still* drunk?"

"Josie."

"Yes?"

"Can you grab me a big bowl from the kitchen? Maybe the garbage can?"

"Oh, shit. She's gonna pop! Candace!"

I heard the cabinet open and the sound of plastic bowls scraping against each other assaulted my ears. Something whisked through the air, *thunked* against Josie's hands, and before I knew it, a five-quart green plastic mixing bowl was shoved in front of my face just as I let loose.

I coughed, sputtered, and hurled until my eyes watered and I moaned, rolling onto my back. Josie's hand had been around my hair the whole time.

"Come on, sweetie. Let's get you into bed."

A pair of hands slipped under my arms and another set wrapped around my knees. Then I was floating. Floating and groaning and bouncing. My stomach lurched, and I burped.

"Don't puke!"

"Not. I done."

"Uh huh."

"Water and Advil. If you could kill me, that would be much appreciated, too."

"Nope. You're going to suffer and I'm going to laugh."

"You're mean in the morning."

"Only when my roommate is dumb enough to get pukey drunk and I have to take care of her."

"Shut up. When was the last time? 87? 88?"

"88 I think. After the Duran Duran concert."

"That was fun. We should do that again."

"I think they broke up a couple of decades ago, sweetie."

"Bummer."

They set me gently on my bed and the room started spinning. I looked down at my feet and found Candace perched there with a worried look on her face.

"Ugh. Kill me now. I don't want to live."

"Watch her. I'm going to go get her some water."

A moment later and Candace was peering at my face. I attempted to smile, but it hurt too much. "Help."

She sighed and touched the tip of her finger to my forehead. "*Bliv bedre*."

A cool feeling spread through my head, the pounding stopped, and so did the spinning room. "Woah."

"Better?"

"Yes. Thank you."

She nodded and sat down next to me, rubbing my tummy. She started singing in a language I had never heard, sounding similar to her spell. "What language is that?"

"Danish."

"That feels good." There was nothing sexual about it either. It was like a mother soothing her child.

I must have dozed off, when I opened my eyes again, she was gone. I gingerly lifted my head off the pillow and gave it a tentative shake. There was no headache rattling around. "Sweet Lady of Light."

I unceremoniously rolled over and got my feet on the floor, facing the bed in case I fell. I really needed to pee. I lifted myself up and stumbled to the bathroom. There might not have been a headache, but I was still hungover.

After I peed, I pulled my leggings off and went from the toilet straight into the shower, standing against the back wall until the water warmed enough to plunge beneath it. Ten minutes later, I was almost human. I would need coffee and water to elevate myself back to witch. I wasn't drinking for another forty years or so.

I washed up and got out of the shower, grabbing a clean towel and drying myself as I wandered back into my bedroom. I tossed the towel on the chest at the end of my bed and pulled an oversized T-shirt out of my dresser. Pulling it over my head I reentered the land of the living.

Chief was gone, or at least not on my couch. It was Monday morning. I'm sure he panicked and ran home to freshen up before heading into work. I just hoped he didn't get a DUI on the way home. I told myself to check on him via text *after* I got some coffee into me.

I put a pot up to brew and shifted from foot to foot as I impatiently waited for my liquid heroin. Five minutes later, I said, "Fuck it," and yanked the pot out while it was still brewing and splashed some in my mug. I'd clean the mess up later. Replacing the pot back under the flow as quickly as I could, I took a swig. I let it roll over my tongue and almost choked on how strong it was.

Oh, well.

I smiled at my mug, the only one who loved me, and went and sat on the couch, folding my legs beneath me as I held my head in my hand and kept sipping the coffee.

The doorbell rang and I didn't even remotely want to get up. "Come in!" I yelled as loud as I could. Either they heard me, or they didn't. I didn't care either way.

The door tried to open, but it was locked. I sighed, and stood up, walking over. I unlocked it and unlatched it, but I wasn't pulling it open. I had to do enough just to get my ass back down on the couch and stop the room from spinning.

"You look like shit." Jimmy's disapproving voice grated on my nerves.

"Thanks. Coincidentally, that's how I feel."

"Coffee?"

"Kitchen."

"Need more?"

"Please," I said and hoisted my mug over my shoulder, not taking my head from my hand.

He sat next to me, offering my freshly filled mug. I breathed it in and took another sip. I might have made some appreciative noises, too. "Thanks."

"Welcome," he said simply and sipped his coffee next to me. "You gonna live?"

"Not sure I want to."

"Oh, come on. Hangovers aren't that bad. Own that shit."

"Go lick an outlet."

"I like your hair."

"Thanks. Grew it last night. Debated going with the purple mohawk."

"That would have been hot."

"Did you actually need something, or did you come to torment me?'

"Little bit of both. I need a date."

"Excuse me?" I finally turned and looked at him.

"I need you. To be my girlfriend tonight."

"Why?"

"My mother is coming into town. She wants to take me to dinner. Us actually."

"Us?"

"I might have mentioned you once or twice."

"To your mother," I said incredulously.

He sighed and set his coffee on the table. "She thinks I'm gay…"

I couldn't help it. I laughed.

"It's not funny. She swears up and down that Dennis and I are lovers. The last time she said it, I kind of mentioned you…"

"Okay." I let him off the hook.

"You will?"

"That's what okay means."

"You are a life saver."

"Jimmy?"

"Yes?"

"Are you and Dennis lovers?" I gave him an evil grin.

He groaned and put his head in his hands, shaking it in agony. "Why does everybody assume that?"

I felt bad for asking, but I didn't want secrets between us. "Well… Let's be honest. You two do spend a *lot* of time together."

"No! We are not. I mean there was that one time in college…"

"What?" My heart fell into my stomach.

"I'm kidding."

"I'm going to kill you," I said and started breathing again.

"Were you jealous of Dennis there for a second?"

Looking into his eyes, my heart skipped a beat as I opened my mouth to say no, I swear to the lady, but I ended up nodding and blushing. He chuckled evilly.

"Good."

"Hey. Are we?" I blushed as the question flew out of my mouth.

"Are we what?"

"Boyfriend and girlfriend?"

"Yes. If you're comfortable with that."

I smiled and lay back on the couch.

"You sure you're going to be up to going out tonight?"

"Oh, I wouldn't miss this for the world."

"Oh, Lady. Don't do anything Dottish. Please. And don't mention Chief."

I snorted. "I don't even want to think of Chief for a few days."

"That bad?"

"No. It would just remind me of last night and if I do that, I might throw up again."

"Um?"

"He came over and we both apologized. Then we sat on the couch and drank until we passed out. I woke up, puked, and the girls carried me into bed."

"Huh. I saw Bill this morning. He looked fine."

"He would. That asshole."

"So. Were you guys…uh…naked?"

"You, too?"

"What?"

"He got all jealous last night."

"Really?"

"Yeah. Must have been the booze."

"No, I'm not jealous. Just curious."

"How can you not be? I thought of you with Dennis for a microsecond and I almost snarled. Do you really not care?" I wanted answers.

Jimmy sighed. "I'm sorry. I didn't mean to upset you." He lowered his eyes.

I reached over and grabbed his chin, forcing his head up until he looked at me again. "Talk to me. I want to know."

"Dot... Don't hate me for saying this, but you..."

"If you don't start talking in eight seconds, I'm going to rip off your junk and beat you with it."

"Dot, it turns me on!"

"Uh... What turns you on?" I sincerely hoped it wasn't the thought of me beating him with his junk.

He sighed, and I could see he was embarrassed and on the verge of tears. "I can't."

"Yes. Yes, you can," I said gently. "I promise not to be shocked or grossed out. What turns you on?"

"The thought of you with someone else."

"Why?" I wasn't shocked. I knew there had to be some sort of explanation other than, *because you're our high priestess and you can have everybody!*

"Because I *really* like you. A lot. Don't worry, I won't drop the L word on you. I know it's too soon, but Lady damn it all, the first moment I saw you I was hooked."

"That doesn't answer my question."

"Because at the end of the day, knowing you were with someone else and you still came back to me... I'm not going to lie, it makes me feel like I'm special and it also makes me hard as a rock."

"Oh. I see," I said and took a sip of coffee, thinking about it. *Really* thinking about it.

"Do you think I'm sick?"

I shook my head, just to let him know I wasn't disgusted by his logic, just mulling it over. It did make sense, in a Jimmy sort of way. I knew a *lot* about fetishes. Hell, Josie was as kinky as they came. Some of the videos she watched would make a porn star blush. People just had their kinks. I wasn't going to make fun of Jimmy for his. "No. That actually answers a lot of questions I had. You were being way too accommodating with me seeing Chief. This actually makes me feel a lot better."

He sighed in relief and lay back against the couch with me. "Be right back, I forgot my coffee. He leaned forward and grabbed it off the table and then leaned back next to me. "Miss me?"

"Horribly."

He chuckled and I lay my head on his shoulder. "Wanna know something else?"

"What?"

"The thought of you being hard as a rock because I'm with another man… Kinda turns me on. Now who's fucked up?"

He laughed wickedly and sipped his coffee. "So, you don't mind being my girlfriend tonight?"

"I don't mind being your girlfriend anytime."

"Thanks for doing this, though. You don't know what a relief it is. She can be so annoying."

"Must be a witch thing. My mother is the biggest pain in the ass in the universe."

"Um. My mother is human…"

"What?"

"Yeah. Dad's a witch. Mom *knows* but is as human as they come."

"How old is she?"

"Fifty-five. Dad is a hundred years older but looks the same age as me. It's kind of funny, everybody thinks Mom is rich."

"They're still together?"

"Yeah. He loves her."

"How come he's not coming?"

"Work. They live in Texas and Dad owns a cattle farm."

"So how come you live here?"

"Mom was born here. Dad was here just wandering. They settled down, got married, had me. Moved to Texas after I graduated from the Fire Academy."

"Huh. That's pretty neat."

"You like them sappy love stories, huh?"

I nodded. "Want some more coffee?"

"I'll get it." He took my mug and got up.

I turned sideways on the couch and pulled my T-shirt over my knees. He came back and sat next to me, almost on my feet, handing me my mug.

"Thanks."

"No. Thank you. I really do feel better. Thank you for making me talk to you."

"I'm a firm believer in not keeping secrets."

"You don't have to worry about that. I want to hear," he said with a sly wink.

I laughed and lifted my legs over him. "So, you want to know that this was exactly how I was sitting on Chief last night?"

He leaned back further on the couch. "What were you wearing."

"Leggings. You saw my outfit last night."

"Aww. That's no fun. You could have spiced it up a little."

"I could tell you about the last time we drank together."

"Did anything interesting happen?"

"Oh, yeah."

"Tell me."

"Well, we were both drunk, though not nearly as much as last night. When we woke up, he was in my bed and we were both naked."

His cock twitched under my leg. He really was getting turned on by it. I smiled wickedly and rubbed it with the back of my leg.

"Did you do anything?"

"When I woke up, I was having very happy dreams. That's when I realized I was straddling his leg and he was pressing against me."

Jimmy groaned a little and his twitch turn into a throb.

"You can take that out of your pants if you want. I don't want you to hurt yourself."

He reached under my legs, unzipping his fly and working himself out through the hole. I could feel the heat from it as it popped out between my calves. I squeezed them together, trapping him between them.

"Oh, Lady."

"So, I can't help myself, I'm incredibly turned on and I start grinding myself subtly against his leg. I thought I was being all slick and covert, but he asked me what I was doing. I tried to play it off like I was just stretching, but he knew. I saw him twitch under the blanket. I couldn't stop myself and I lifted the cover up and looked. Have you ever seen it?"

"What?" He asked breathlessly.

"Chief's cock."

"No. I know the whole Captain Nightstick thing… Is it really?"

"It is."

"Did you touch it?"

"I poked it."

A short bark of laughter escaped him. "You poked it?"

"Yeah, but I told him I wasn't comfortable touching it while I was dating you."

Jimmy groaned in disappointment.

"I'm not done with my story. So, I get so slick I start sliding up and down his thigh, then I tell him I want to watch him rub one out and come on his chest."

"Did he?"

"He started to, and then I helped. We were both rubbing his cock when I came so hard on his leg, I thought I was going to pass out."

"What did Chief do?"

"He came. Buckets. I screamed so hard from my orgasm, Josie and Candace burst into my room wielding a kitchen knife."

Jimmy had heard enough. He came between my legs. I'd been rubbing him and not realizing it. His hot come landed all over my shins. Incredibly turned on, I opened my legs and reached down, running my middle finger through my wetness, right in front of him. His eyes fixated on me as I masturbated right in front of him. The only time he stopped was to watch my face every few moments.

"Put your finger in me."

He reached over, slipping his first two fingers inside and curling them up, sliding them in and out gently as I rubbed myself. My breaths started coming faster and faster as my back slowly arched, and my toes curled. I called out as I came and bucked my hips against his fingers as I rode it out. I finally came down and watched as he slowly pulled his fingers from inside me and sucked them into his mouth.

CHAPTER 4

Pulling into a spot at Bunyan's steakhouse, I looked around for Jimmy's truck in the lot. He hadn't shown up yet, but Chief's new Jeep was here.

Oh, shit. There's like ten restaurants in this town and he has to have a hankering for steak?

So much for not mentioning Chief in front of his mother…

I debated going inside to wait, but I decided against it. Jimmy had asked me not to mention him to his mother, so waiting outside sounded like a better plan than hanging out with Chief until they showed up. Even if it was cold as fuck. With any luck he was just finishing his prime rib and would soon be on his way.

I chose wisely, as Jimmy's pristine blue Ford pulled into the lot shortly after I shut the engine off. I was facing the entrance to the parking lot and flashed my headlights to let him know I was there in the car. He pulled into the empty spot next to mine.

I got out, pulling my fuzzy winter coat tightly around me. I'd worn a simple black dress, going for broke in impressing the mother. I couldn't even remember the last time I'd tried to impress anybody, let alone a date's parents. Hopefully she would appreciate my dressing up a little. Unfortunately, it did little to keep me warm.

As soon as the engine stopped, the nervousness I hadn't realized I'd been feeling, reared its ugly head. I fought down a bit of panic until Jimmy got out of the truck and gave me a quick kiss. He flashed me a little grin before he walked around the truck and opened the passenger door for his mother, offering her his hand to help ease the difficulty of getting out.

"I wish you'd buy a damn car," his mother snarked as her feet hit the pavement.

"I tell him all the time, too. I hate riding in that damn thing," I said to break the ice.

"Oh! You must be Dot!"

"And you must be Mrs. Duncan. Pleasure to meet you. Jimmy talks a lot about you."

"I'm sure he does. I'm not all that bad, though."

"Well, we'll talk over dinner and compare notes. I'm interested in what he's had to say about me, too." I even threw in a conspiratorial little wink.

She turned to Jimmy. "How in the hell did you land her? You tell her you work for NASA or something?"

"Funny, Mother. Shall we go inside?"

"Hell yeah. I forgot how cold it is in this state. Don't know how you put up with it."

Jimmy flashed me a smile of gratitude for pouring on the charm with his mother. "Thanks," he whispered, holding my hand as his mother scurried to the entrance to warm her bones.

"I hope the food's good here."

"It is, Mother."

"I'm used to Texas beef, you know."

"You might have mentioned that, yes."

"Tenderest beef in the country."

"So, I've heard." He leaned over. "Repeatedly," he whispered to me.

I stifled a chuckle and wrapped myself around his arm. "She's right, though. It is cold as balls."

I happened to glance up at the window as we passed by. Chief was sitting there at the table we had shared and gave me a small wave. I gave him a quick nod and smile.

"There's Bill," Jimmy said and waved.

"Yeah. I saw his Jeep parked out front."

"Have you ever been here before?"

"Yeah. Once with Bill."

"Ahh. I come with Dennis a lot. They have really good steak."

"Not better than Texas steak, though," I whispered and bumped his hip.

We got inside, and I could breathe again. The warmth wrapped around me like a blanket. I shrugged my jacket off and Jimmy took it, hanging it and his on the rack before taking his mother's. The hostess sat us, and the waitress popped over to take our drink orders. The thought of beer or wine caused my stomach to twist in a knot, so I ordered a coke.

"So, what do you do, dear?"

"I'm building a bookstore downtown. In the old firehouse if you remember where that is."

"In this dump?"

"Trying to revitalize this dump. Breathe some new life into it."

"You're a do-gooder?"

"No. I just want to enjoy the town I live in."

"Mother," Jimmy warned.

"What?"

"Not everybody outside of Texas is a hippie. Dot just has a big heart. Too big sometimes," he said and gave me a tender smile.

"I just like helping people." I think I may have even blushed when I said it.

He reached down and rubbed my leg. I glanced up. From where we were sitting in our booth, I could see Chief. He was absentmindedly chewing his steak and scrolling through his phone. He looked up, saw me staring, and tipped his beer at me.

The waitress showed up with drinks and blocked my view, thankfully. It wasn't that I minded seeing him. However, seeing him while actually *being* on a date made

41

me feel awkward. I didn't have to hide, but I kind of wanted to. I scooted closer to Jimmy, enjoying his warmth and cologne. He smelled good enough to eat.

"Are you ready to order or do you need a few more minutes."

"I'm ready," I told Jimmy.

"I suppose we're ready," his mother told the girl, answering for the whole table. "I'll have the porterhouse, medium well, loaded potato, and the baby carrots."

She looked to me. "And for you?"

"Prime rib, princess cut, medium rare, potato with butter only, and the mushrooms."

"Sir?"

"I'll have the same, but the king cut."

"Sounds good. I'll have everything out to you shortly."

She left and Jimmy nervously started rubbing my leg. An awkward silence fell over us and Jimmy cleared his throat, clearly nervous being there with his mother. I just didn't know what I could do to help. Taking a sip of my coke, I snuggled a little closer to him, trying to set him at ease.

"So, what was little Jimmy like as a kid?" I figured that would be a nice safe topic.

"He was a little trouble maker." She leaned over the table and whispered, "And him being a you-know-what didn't help at all, either."

"I can only imagine."

"No. You can't. I had to put out twelve fires in the house before he was eight! I didn't think my heart would take it. Thankfully, his father stuck around to help."

"Oh, boy. I'll have to introduce you to my mother. That sounds tame compared to me." I laughed.

"Is your mother…"

"Yes. Father, too. Although, I've never met him."

"Your poor mother raised you by herself?"

"If you met my mother, you wouldn't feel sorry for her. She's worse than I am."

"No!"

"Her most recent endeavor got her in a bit of trouble as she magicked a horse's bunghole on the mayor's forehead. Luckily it was cosmetic in appearance only and not a fully functioning model."

Jimmy's mom started cackling across from us. Jimmy rubbed my leg affectionately. I glanced over at Chief and he was putting another forkful of food in his mouth as he stared at me. I cocked my eyebrow at him, but he wasn't looking at my face. His eyes were glued to my rising dress. If Jimmy continued, I'm sure he would have a nice view of the front of my white lace panties.

"I'll be right back. I need to use the little cowgirl's room."

"Okay, Mom," Jimmy smiled. He watched her slide out of the booth and head toward the other side of the restaurant. "Oh, thank the Lady. You okay?"

"Yeah. She's fine. Nothing compared to my mother. Whom you shall have the pleasure of dining with next time *she* is in town."

He groaned.

"Uh, Jimmy?"

"Yes?"

"You might want to stop with the leg rubbing, you're giving Chief quite the show."

"What?"

I turned to face him and put my head on my hand. "You've been slowly hiking my dress up. Chief is sitting diagonally from me and can probably see right up it. So, you might want to stop."

"Hmm. I might. But then again, I might not…"

"You're evil."

"But fun at parties."

I chuckled. "Well, I'm sure *he* doesn't mind."

I sat back in my seat and took another sip of coke. I hoped the waitress hurried with the food, I was actually hungry. I gasped when Jimmy reach down and slowly dragged the hem of my dress up a little higher.

"Spread your legs."

"Did you forget we are having dinner with your *mother*?"

"She can't see. Shh. Here she comes."

Mrs. Duncan slid back into the booth. "Well, that's better."

"Welcome back," I said sweetly and tried to ignore Jimmy pulling my left leg closer to him. I gave up and let him have his way, but not daring to look in Chief's direction.

"Thank you, dear. So, what did I miss?"

"Just your son, being your son."

"That bad, huh?"

"Nah. Jimmy is sweet. A little on the strange side, but I like that about him."

"I will say, Dot. You aren't at all what I was expecting."

"In what way?" I said, truly curious. Jimmy's hand began rubbing the inside of my thigh before stopping. His fingers began caressing the soft flesh instead, slowly dragging up and down. I truly didn't mean to, but I happened to glance up at Chief. He had completely forgotten his meal and was openly staring. I got the shock of my life when I realized how much it was turning me on.

"Honestly, he described you as some sort of goddess."

I snorted. "That couldn't be farther from the truth."

"Not that I disagree with him, you are quite beautiful. But you have this down to earth feel about you, too."

"Aww. Thank you, Mrs. Duncan," I said and meant it. For all his complaining, she was very sweet. "Usually people just tell me I'm scary."

"I can see that, too," she said with a wink. "But, please, call me Peggy."

"All right. If you insist."

Jimmy's fingers slid closer to the front of my panties. If he thought he was going to touch me there with his mother at the table, I was going to break his fingers.

Luckily, he stopped short, putting his head on his other hand and talking to his mother. "She really can be. You should see her when she's angry."

"I can imagine."

I ignored the irony of his statement and looked back over at Chief. He was feasting on the view, still. I couldn't stop myself. I shifted in my seat again, turning a little more toward him and opening my legs a little bit more as I leaned against Jimmy's shoulder. His hand didn't stop teasing me, either. In fact, I think he knew what I was doing and got a tad bit bolder. Not sticking his fingers in my panties, but "accidentally" bumping into them with his pinky.

The waitress brought our food, unfortunately.

"Well, it certainly *looks* delicious." Peggy said grudgingly.

I nodded at her steak. "I had that the last time I was here. I think you'll be impressed."

I grabbed my knife and fork and cut a piece off my prime rib. I'd thought the porterhouse was tender, the rib was heaven. I closed my eyes and chewed. "Wow."

"Yeah. Their prime rib is tough to beat. Want to try it, Mom?"

"Cut me off a little piece."

I finished chewing and opened my eyes. Chief had been watching me with a little smile on his face. I gave him a little wink and mixed the butter into my potato, pouring a half a ton of salt onto it and a bit more on my meat. Jimmy's elbow bumped into me as he cut his.

"Sorry, sweetie," I said and scooted over, giving him a little bit more room.

"No worries, hon," he said and grinned at me.

"You two are just too cute. Stop it. I'm trying to eat."

I gave Peggy a little chuckle and took another bite. I seriously wanted to groan. It was that good. Chief had resumed eating his steak, only casually glancing my way. I knew because I'd been watching him from the corner of my eye.

Jimmy must have too because he paused eating, said something to his mother and put his hand on my leg, again. He nudged me to open them and then picked his fork back up. I got the hint. He wanted me to continue my show. Jimmy had certainly come out of his shell.

I figured, what the hell. It wasn't anything Chief hadn't seen before. He didn't seem to mind watching, either. I shifted in my seat, pretending to rearrange myself as I lifted my dress a tad higher, nothing obscene, but just enough. Taking another bite of food, I lifted my eyes and they met Chief's. He narrowed his eyes and they didn't leave mine. I slowly opened my legs and watched his expression. His eyes flickered down, and his eyebrow lifted. He knew I had to be doing it on purpose.

I continued eating, slowly opening and closing them the entire time. When I finished, I pushed my plate forward a little and scooted back toward Jimmy. We were done, but his mother was still working on her meal. I didn't know if she was going to finish or not.

"She's got a healthy appetite," she said as she took another piece of steak.

"Yeah. I eat a *lot*. Everybody teases me about it."

"Well, as long as it doesn't go straight to your ass, enjoy it."

"I do."

She chuckled. "I think I'm about done. That was very good, I'm impressed."

Chief got up from his booth, finished with his meal. He strolled past us, muttering an, "Evening, folks."

"Hey, Chief."

He didn't stop to chat, just kept walking. I couldn't tell if he was upset or not. I'd find out later, I'm sure. He wasn't exactly a hold it in kind of person.

The waitress stopped by our table again. "Can I get you folks any dessert?"

"No, thank you. I think we're stuffed." Jimmy paused to shoot me a quick glance, but I shook my head. I *was* stuffed. She picked up our plates and ran them back to the kitchen, returning quickly with our check. Jimmy reached for it, but I snagged it.

"Hey, I asked you to dinner," he protested.

"And I accepted and paid. Suck it up."

I slipped my bank card into the leather holder with the check, setting it on the edge of the table for the waitress to pick it up.

"I like her. You better keep her."

"I think it's more of a question of her keeping me."

"What?" Jimmy's answer kind of struck me as sad. "Why wouldn't I?"

"It was a joke, Dot."

"Okay. But don't make jokes like that."

"Men. Always so insecure."

"I know right?" I nodded at Peggy.

"I am not! Dot is just…"

"Oh, would you take me off the damn pedestal already. It's getting kind of annoying."

"Now you two are just ganging up on me."

"Of course, we are. You have a penis and are our mortal enemy."

He squeezed my knee and I jumped. "You deserved that."

"I might have," I said and smiled after I stopped squirming. I signed the bill and we headed out after grabbing our coats. "How long will you be in town, Peggy?"

"I'm leaving in the morning. I just flew in to check on this dolt. He told me he was in the hospital. Just had to see him with my own eyes."

"Yeah. Mine did the same thing when my car blew up."

Jimmy squeezed my hand and coughed.

"Your car…blew up?"

"Yeah. Defect with the gas tank. Luckily, the airbags deployed and shielded me from most of it. Magic took care of the rest."

"Oh. Okay. I'm glad you weren't hurt."

"Here's the keys, Mom. I'm going to say goodnight to Dot. Be there in minute."

"Okay, Junior."

"Junior?"

"No. Don't ever," he told me very seriously.

"Well, g'night, Dot. Thanks for a wonderful dinner."

"It was nice meeting you, Peggy. Hope to see you again soon."

"I'll be back for Christmas. Big Jim, too."

I assumed Big Jim was Jimmy's father, hence the Junior. I tried not to chuckle as she gave me a quick hug and wandered toward the truck.

Jimmy took his turn and wrapped me in his arms, giving me a solid kiss that warmed me more than the jacket. He didn't let go either. "Did you like that?"

"Meeting your mother? Yes. She was very sweet."

"You know damn well what I'm talking about, Dot." He laughed, and I felt it more in his chest than heard it.

"You showing me to Chief? Very much so. You should be more concerned if he liked it."

"I'm sure he enjoyed the view."

"Not what I'm talking about. I meant more of you showing me off."

"Oh. Was he mad?"

"I'm not sure, but I'll let you know. I'm sure I'll hear about it either way."

"Please do." He chuckled again.

"Go. Mama's waitin', Junior."

"Oh, no. Please don't," he whined.

"Okay. I won't. Unless you piss me off."

"Deal. See you tomorrow?"

"I have no plans. Want to come over for dinner?"

"Okay, but I get to buy this time. Chinese?"

"Sounds good." I lifted myself up on my toes and kissed him again.

"And thanks for going with us tonight. It meant a lot to me," he added before pulling away and heading toward his truck.

I watched him walk away and couldn't help the smile that crawled up from my heart and settled on my face. Jimmy might be full of quirks, but I could honestly say there wasn't a minute spent with him that I didn't enjoy. He even brought me coffee when I needed it.

CHAPTER 5

I shouldn't have been surprised to see Chief's Jeep in my driveway, but I was. Apprehensively, I pulled into the spot next to him and killed the engine. I sat there for a full minute before finally building up enough courage to go inside.

He was sitting on my couch, drinking a beer and watching sports highlights on the television. He didn't have the sound on and I'm not sure he was actually watching.

"Hey, Bill."

"Dot."

Tossing my jacket on the rack, I headed to the kitchen. I'd pledged to never drink again too soon. I needed something to take the edge off the anxiety that had been building in my chest since dinner. Grabbing one out of the fridge, I cooled it off and popped the top, taking a long swig before plopping down on the loveseat across from him.

"Whatcha up to?"

"Having a beer."

"Josie home?"

"In her room."

"Candace at work?"

"Yup."

"You pissed?"

"A little."

I sighed, grateful to get to the point.

"I'm sorry."

He kind of gave me a shocked look. "Look. I don't mind that you're also dating Jimmy, we've been over that. I wouldn't even have minded seeing you out on a date, I should expect that. It is a small town, but…"

"We went overboard."

"Yes. But nice panties, by the way."

"I'm sorry."

"I know it was just Jimmy flaunting you off to me to grind my gears, but…"

If this was going to work, I needed to be honest with him. "That's not it."

"What isn't?"

"He didn't do it to make you mad."

"Why the hell would he flip up your skirt then?"

"To turn you on. Jimmy…likes that I'm seeing you. It kind of does it for him, if you know what I mean."

"What?"

"Lady Light, Chief. Do I have to spell it out?"

"Apparently…"

"Jimmy gets turned on not being the only man in my life."

"What? Why?"

"Why do people get turned on by feet? Or nuns? Nobody knows. People like what they like, and Jimmy likes me seeing other guys. Namely you. He didn't do it to make you mad, he was being…nice?"

"And how do you feel about it?"

I shrugged my shoulders.

"Be honest."

"It turns me on, too."

"Really?"

I shrugged again.

"Why, or more specifically, what turns you on about it?"

"A few things. I like both you and Jimmy a *lot*. If I *had* to choose one of you, I don't think I could. But, I also like the fact that me fooling around with you excites him. I guess I'm weird, too."

"I didn't say you were weird. Jimmy, maybe. I don't mind you fooling around with him, but I try not to think about it, either. It makes me growly if I do."

"Why?"

"I don't know. I know I don't have a right to be, but I am. Must be a caveman thing."

"Want to know something else?"

"I don't know, do I?"

I nodded my head and lifted my knees, letting my dress slip down my thighs. "It also turns me on that you get growly thinking of me with Jimmy…"

Chief's eyes fixated on the front of my panties. "Does teasing me turn you on?"

"Very much…"

That was all it took, he stood, walked around the coffee table and knelt in front of me, gently kissing the front of my panties. "You smell amazing."

"Guys are weird."

"Why?" He looked up at me.

"Some like the taste, some like the smell, some like both."

"I'm a both kind of guy." He lightly ran his tongue up the front of them, pushing the gusset into my lips. I sighed and lay back, letting him take the reins.

He pulled his face back and lightly ran his knuckles over me, causing me to quiver. "Is there anything else that turns you on?"

I thought about it. Thought about how I felt in the restaurant. Thought about how I felt when Dennis had been listening to Jimmy and I fool around. "Apparently, I like to be watched."

"How?" He switched from knuckles to finger and ran it over my panties, swirling through the wetness that had already collected. I had a feeling they were going to get much worse.

"You watching me as Jimmy caressed my thigh. Dennis listening to Jimmy and I fool around… I didn't know I liked an audience until recently. Hell, it even turned me on when Josie burst into my bedroom on us the other morning."

He pulled the front of my panties to the side and ran his tongue over me. I gasped and grabbed a fistful of cushion as I fought not to scream.

"Lady Light, you taste amazing." He went down on me fervently, parting my lips and using his tongue to lap every bit of wetness away. "What else?"

"Jimmy asked what you and I had done. I told him about the other morning… Oh, my goddess. That. Yes."

"Did you tell him?" He asked as he used his fingers to push back my hood, exposing my most sensitive part as he lightly ran the length of his tongue gently across it and then used the tip to rub the flesh around it.

"You're going to make me come."

"That's the plan."

"Yes. Yes, I told him. I told him every little detail. I told him how I helped you jerk your cock. I told him about grinding my pussy against your leg. I told him how we came…"

His tongue dove inside me. I squealed as the beginnings of my orgasm rushed up from the very hole he was diving in. My hips began to grind me against his face as he pulled me against him.

"Fuck, fuck, fuck," was all I could breathlessly moan. My head lifted from the back of the couch to watch him. I wanted to see his face as I came, buried in me.

I almost gasped when I saw Josie standing in the kitchen with a hungry in her eyes. When she saw me looking at her, she blushed and tiptoed quietly into her room.

I hadn't been lying to him when I said it turned me on when Josie burst in my room. Her standing there, watching

Chief go down on me, caused a shudder to well up inside me as my orgasm peaked...

"Fuuuuck," I moaned as it raced through me, my hips heaving involuntarily as I curled upward and shuddered, unable to breathe or see as I convulsed. Through it all, Chief had never let me go and let me slowly come down from the high wracking every nerve in my body. He pulled his tongue out and I spasmed as I fought to control my breathing. Quivering as my orgasm threatened to return.

Chief crawled up me and kissed me. He had unceremoniously wiped his face off first, for which I was grateful, but I could still smell me on his lips. His kiss was tender and grateful. "That was amazing."

"Yes, you were. Thank you."

"My pleasure."

"No. Pretty sure it was mine."

His laugh sent more shivers through me. He really needed to stop, I didn't know how much more I could take. Finally, he pulled away, sitting back down on the couch. He was straining against his jeans, bulging the material over his thigh.

I wanted to pull it out and take it inside me, I really did. But, I wasn't ready yet. He was more than special to me, but deep down, that would have made it too real. I'd just admitted earlier, that Jimmy was my boyfriend. It might take a while for me to admit it again, and I think he knew that as he didn't seem to be expecting anything more. I couldn't leave him like that, though.

"Take your jeans off."

"Pardon?"

"You're really going to make me ask again?"

"No. But, you really don't have to..."

"I know. I *want* to."

He didn't need to be coaxed any more than that. Without standing up, he unbuckled his belt and popped the button, sliding them down with his boxers.

He sprang upward, slapping himself in the stomach before it poised straight up in the air.

"Scoot down on the couch more."

He slid lower in his seat, his ass nearly hanging off the couch.. I wasn't ready to fuck him, but I could definitely make him come.

I got up from the couch, shucking my dress on the floor, I wasn't wearing a bra and left my panties on, just as a last bastion of resistance. I stepped over his thighs and sat down on his lap facing him, his cock nestled against my wet panties. Leaning back a little, I rubbed it against me, moving it from side to side, letting his heat warm my flesh as I began to pump him with my hand.

I enjoyed the feeling as much as he did. He needed a little lubrication. I pulled back a little and let go of him as I was using my other hand to balance myself on his leg. I reached into my panties and began rubbing myself, bucking as my hand reignited the spasms that had finally subsided. I sighed as I tore my hand away and wrapped it back around his shaft, pulling him against me again. My hand glided over him, concentrating on the tip. He reached out and fingered my nipple before reaching down and pulling the excess skin tight on his cock. I stared into his eyes as I jerked him. I could feel my orgasm building again just from the friction of him on my clit. I was unsure of who was going to go first.

I smiled as I caught him staring at me, smiling. My heart might have skipped a beat or two until his breathing quickened and he closed his eyes, his hips undulating beneath me.

"Dot..." He was warning me, and I didn't care. I wanted to feel his heat on my skin. I pumped faster and began grinding my hips harder.

He erupted, painting my flesh white. It ran over my chest and down between my breasts, a channel flowing between us.

As soon as it touched my already wet flesh, I shuddered and cried out, too. Unable to support myself, I leaned forward against him. One thing was for certain, we needed a shower and I needed to reassess my feelings for Chief. I saw the look he had been giving me while we'd been fooling around, and it wasn't just lust.

I'm sure he saw the same thing on my face.

∞ ∞ ∞

I waved goodbye one last time and shut the door behind me, leaning against it for support. Thankfully I had dressed in my terrycloth robe after we got out of the shower or I'd have been frozen solid by the gust of arctic wind blowing in through the door. It had started snowing again and didn't show any signs of slowing.

"Is he gone?"

"Yep." I went to the kitchen and poured a couple glasses of wine, handing one to Josie as she came out of her room.

"Dot…"

I held up my hand, not really wanting to talk about it.

"You mad?"

I shook my head.

"You are mad."

"No, Josie. I'm not mad. Don't worry about it. Just kind of uncomfortable. If we could *never* talk about it, I would appreciate it."

"Okay." She took a sip of her wine. "It was hot though."

"Josie!"

"What? It was. I couldn't help myself."

"I was going to let you watch again, too. But now you ruined it," I said and shook my head, draining half of my glass in one gulp.

"Really?"

"No."

"You suck."

"Actually, I didn't."

"I know…"

I nearly choked on my wine. "You were watching then, too?"

She sheepishly nodded, laughing into her glass. "I just didn't do it in the middle of the kitchen this time."

I was speechless. I guess I was partially to blame. If I wanted privacy, I shouldn't have made out with my boyfriend in the living room. That, and I truly liked it, but I wasn't going to tell *her* that. I'd never have privacy again.

"You promise you're not mad?"

"I promise," I reiterated.

"Okay. Can I ask you a question?"

"You just did."

"Seriously, are you twelve?"

"What is your question?"

"Do you think I should tell Candace I was watching the two of you?"

"I think if you didn't and she ever found out, you would break her little heart."

"Yeah. I'll tell her."

"Good girl. You really like her don't you." I could tell. I just wanted to hear it from her.

"Yes! I really do. And not just when we–"

"Too much information." I laughed as I cringed.

"Sorry."

"No, you're not."

"I can draw you pictures…"

"I can turn you into hamburger…" I mimicked her tone perfectly. I'd perfected it over the years.

She chuckled and took another drink. "So yeah. That was pretty hot."

"Thanks. He is…"

"Yeah. And a bag of chips. That thing is pretty amazing."

"Shut up!" I threw a pillow at her and gasped when I forgot she had a glass of wine.

"*Confuto,*" she said and held out her hand, giving me a dirty look.

I breathed again when the pillow floated harmlessly to the floor. "Thanks."

The doorbell rang. "Candace?"

"Too early and she has a key."

"Maybe it's Jimmy?"

"Lady help you if it is. You gonna be *sore.*"

"Shut up!" I set my wine down, got up, and padded to the door, twisting the lock and pulling it open without looking through the peephole.

I gasped.

Amir held a beautiful blonde covered in gaping wounds. He panted heavily as he swayed back and forth in my doorway. "Help us, please, " he croaked and passed out on my floor.

CHAPTER 6

"What do we do? Can we even heal a vampire?"

We had dragged them into the spare bedroom and gotten them onto the bed. We put Amir closest to the wall, he didn't look half as bad as the female vampire he'd been carrying. "I don't know, but we can try…"

"You try it. I'm not gonna try it. And Mikey ain't here."

"Shut up! Let me think."

I ran my finger of one of the heavier wounds on her arm. She wore a sleeveless leather jerkin, a heavy leather skirt, and boots that laced up all the way to her knees. She looked like an escapee from a renaissance fair. At least she didn't move when I touched her. She was completely dead to the world. I just didn't have any way to tell if she was truly dead. Vampires didn't breathe, nor did they have a pulse. I could only try and hope for the best.

I poured a bit of power into the wound and called out, "*Leigheas an comhlacht, é a dhéanamh go hiomlán.*" I knew it hadn't worked even before I moved my fingers. When I used magic, the power *went* somewhere, changing my intent into reality. When I tried to heal the vampire, the power came back. "Shit."

"Maybe don't *heal* her?"

"What?"

"Fix her, don't heal her."

"That doesn't make any sense."

"Think about it. Would you *heal* a car? No. You'd fix it. Use that as your intent and see what happens."

61

I rolled my eyes and did what she said. "*Dún.*"

I could almost hear her flesh sizzle as the wound bubbled and closed. I watched her face, seeing no signs of pain or discomfort. I looked up at Josie. "You're almost brilliant."

"Thanks. I think."

"Help me."

"You want me to touch her?"

"Yes! Close the wounds on her legs. I'll do the rest."

It took over an hour, but we finally did it. She wouldn't lose any more blood, but if she woke up, that would be a different story. Amir had far fewer wounds. How the hell he had carried her all the way from Canada blew my mind.

I collapsed to the floor against the wall by the door. "Holy hell, I'm tired."

"What time is it?"

"Beats the hell out of me. The sun isn't up yet."

"Um…"

"Shit!"

"Is that even true?"

"Do you want to chance it?"

"Not after all the work we did."

I got up and walked over to the window, leaning in and whispering to the glass, "*Bí i do chloch.*" The glass became opaque, then brownish-gray as it rearranged its molecules into granite. "There. That should do it. No sunlight getting through there."

"You're so…handy."

I sat back down on the ground, thinking about our new guests. "The sun's not up. They *should* be awake. Maybe they need to feed?"

"Maybe you're off your rocker. Where you gonna get a bear this time of night? Think they might miss one at the zoo if that's what you're thinking."

"No. Not…exactly," I muttered, avoiding Josie's gaze.

"Oh, hell no."

"Just a nibble."

"Dot. If you do this, I will call your mother."

"If you call my mother, I'll call yours."

"And tell her what?"

"*Everything.*"

"As I said, be careful," she said curtly.

"Hit 'em with a binding spell if this goes south. They might not be with it when they wake up. *Don't* hurt them. They did come to us for help."

"Yeah, yeah. But if you sprout fangs, I'm staking you."

"Perv."

"Seriously, I am against this. Be careful."

"Yolo."

"Yeah, pretty sure nobody says that anymore. Ever."

I looked at my wrist and sighed. Standing up, I walked over to the female vampire. I'm pretty sure Amir had mentioned her name, but I couldn't remember what it was.

Yvonne? Yvette? Something like that.

"Alright, Yvonnette... I hope this helps. *Gearr.*" I winced as a cut opened up across my wrist.

"That's so gross I may barf."

Ignoring her, I let the first few drops fall onto the vampire's lips. Immediately her tongue darted out and wiped the crimson liquid off. Going for broke, I carefully put my wrist to her mouth, not wanting to get blood on the comforter.

She suckled like a newborn at first and then her arms reached up faster than my eyes could follow and pressed my arm to her open mouth. Her fangs pierced my skin and I yelped.

Josie surged forward, spell upon her lips, but I held out my hand. "Oh. Oh wow."

"Does it hurt a lot?"

"No. It feels...um. Josie. It feels like sex."

"What? Ew."

"Yes." I tried to ignore it, but it got stronger the longer she fed. After a couple of minutes, I was panting heavy and trying to stand upright. Any more and I'd be writhing on the floor. "Okay, that's enough," I said and pulled my arm away from her mouth.

Reluctantly, she let me go. "Thank the Lady." Josie sounded relieved.

"Woah," I sat down on the bed and shook my head.

The vampire's eyes opened and darted around the room as she did a vampire sit up. She didn't struggle, she didn't use her arms for leverage, the top half of her body just sort of floated up in a ninety-degree angle.

"Relax. You're okay. Amir brought you here earlier. I closed your wounds."

She looked down at her arms, turning them over and inspecting. "You fed me?"

"Um…yeah. You weren't waking up so…"

She turned and looked down at Amir. She gently caressed his cheek and looked him over. "I must hunt to find him food."

"Josie, go see what time it is."

"Be right back."

"It's pretty late. I don't know when the sun will be up."

She nodded.

"Do you really burn in sunlight?"

She nodded again.

"Bummer."

"Bummer?"

"Yeah. That sucks."

"What sucks? Me?"

"You haven't been around people much have you."

She shook her head.

"They're colloquialisms. Bummer and that sucks means…that's horrible."

"Ahh. I see."

"It's almost four in the morning," Josie said. "Candace gets off shortly. Want me to see if she can snag some vampire juice pouches from the hospital?"

"Vampire juice pouches?"

"Bags of human blood."

"Pardon?" The vampire blinked in utter confusion.

"Yes, Josie. Please. Tell her not to get in trouble, but if she can… Tell her I'll make her cookies for dinner."

"Ha. You're trying to fatten up my girlfriend. Lady knows she needs it," she mumbled and walked off to call her.

"Thank you," the vampire humbly said and bowed her head to me.

"You're welcome. What is your name?"

"Yvette."

Ha! I was close.

"Yvette, I'm Dot. Where is the rest of your clan?"

Her face darkened. "Gone. Amir had returned to us to tell us your proposal for moving here and living in sanctuary. Many did not find this…appealing. But he argued for the merits of safety. The coven of witches became bold, attacking our village. They took six of us. Only Amir and I were able to escape."

"They are not witches, they are rogues practicing black magic forbidden to us by the Lady herself." I let the anger into my voice. Yvette backed up as much as she could in the bed and Amir woke. She placed her hand on his arm.

"We are safe," she spoke softly. "You saved us."

"Your wounds."

She nodded at me and he bowed his thanks.

"Well, get some rest. I'll let you know if our friend was able to get some blood from the hospital."

"Like you spoke to me of before? The blood bank?"

"Yes."

He nodded his head. "Thank you."

"You're welcome. Let me know if you need anything. Help yourself to a shower."

They looked at each other in confusion.

This was going to be harder than I thought.

I left them to rest and found Josie in the living room, sitting on the couch. "You're in deep shit, you know that, right?"

"How am I in trouble?"

"How do you think everybody is going to react when they find out you just rented a room to a couple of vampires?"

"They can get over it. What the hell else was I supposed to do?"

"Rent a room at Farrell's? Let Bill set them up a room at the police station where they have–I don't know–guns?"

"He'll bitch, but he'll come around."

"Not just referring to Chief here, Dot. You should have talked to everybody. Even Candace doubts the sanity of your decision."

"What did she say?"

"Was that wise?"

"That sounds like Candace."

"I know. Right?"

The front door lock clicked. "Speaking of the little devil."

We were both staring when she walked in, big fluffy pink jacket bundled around her leaving her purple surgical scrub pants visible from the knees down. She stopped in the doorway and blinked. "What?"

"We were just talking about you."

Her eyes got really big and she looked like she was going to cry. "Oh, sweetie. We were saying nice things about you. And how you think Dot is insane for having the vampires stay here."

"I did not!"

Josie startled laughing.

"You're mean." I slapped her leg.

Candace narrowed her eyes at her as she walked around the sofa, not taking her jacket off. She started pulling bags of blood out of the pockets and handing them to me one by one. "I did not know how much they would need, so I brought lots."

"And nobody is going to miss these?"

She shook her head. "I took them from the storage unit in the ER. They go through a lot and forget to fill out paperwork all the time. I figured that was the safest."

"Bless you, Candace. And thank you."

She nodded and smiled brightly. Only when I had a stack of pouches in my hands did she remove her coat. Her scrubs, since she worked in the pediatric ward, had little pink and blue animal shapes on a purple background that matched the pants. She was adorable.

"How was work?" Josie asked her.

"Sad. I hate seeing sick children. I heal when I can, but I think Doctor Shapiro is watching me."

"Be careful," I said. I trusted the good doctor, but only so far. He knew Josie and I were witches, but I didn't think it was safe to out the whole coven to him…yet.

"Yeah. Don't let the human doctor know you have superpowers, but go ahead and sleep next to a couple of vampires that Dot just met." Josie nodded her head emphatically.

"Leave the sarcasm to the professionals, Josie. Don't want you to hurt yourself."

"Oh, you're funny."

"Candace thinks so."

She was covering her mouth and snickering.

"Well, until we know for sure, you just earned a couple more bunk mates. We're sleeping in your room."

I sighed. It was a small price to pay. At least Candace didn't snore. "Fine. I'm going to take some blood to our guests."

"I'm going to take a shower." Candace headed off to her and Josie's room.

"I'm going to sit here and have another glass of wine and contemplate my best friend's sanity," Josie quipped snottily.

If I wasn't holding ten bags of blood, I would have flipped her off over my shoulder. I headed for the guest room and lightly tapped the door with my foot.

A moment later and Yvette opened the door, eyes widening at the contents of my hands. "Surely…"

"Yep. How much do you need?"

"One should be more than enough. I hate to see the rest turn rancid…"

"It's okay. I'll put it in the… Fuck. My fridge is broken."

"Fridge?"

"It keeps things cold. Stops them from spoiling."

"I do not understand but shall take your word for it."

I handed her two of the bags, thought about it, and handed her a third. "Split the third one or give it to Amir. He might need a little more. I'm going to run this…to a friend's house."

She nodded. "Thank you."

"You can lock the door from the inside. If you need anything else, just ask Josie."

"The one who is against us staying here."

"Yeah. That one." I felt bad. She wasn't upset, but she was a vampire. She probably heard every word Josie said. "Don't worry, you are welcome here."

"I understand her distrust. We were being hunted by witches and asked witches for help. It is hard to know who to trust, and who not to. We chose those not seeking our lives."

"Good choice."

Yvette laughed, sending shivers down my spine just as Amir's had when I first met him. I doubted I would ever get used to it.

"Well, I better get going. Have a good rest."

She leaned forward and kissed me on my forehead. "Night's blessings on you."

"Lady's blessings on you." I said, not knowing what else to say to her. I hoped she wasn't offended by my invocation of our goddess.

She seemed surprised but nodded her thanks before slowly closing the door. I heard the lock click and nodded.

"Josie, grab me a bag, I gotta take the rest of this to… Shit!"

"What?"

"I was going to take it to Jimmy's, but his mother is there. If I start pounding on the door at five in the morning with bags of blood…"

"Gosh. I guess you're going to have to take it to Chief's then, huh?"

"Oh, my Lady, you can be such a bitch."

"Pot, this is Mrs. Kettle. Mrs. Kettle, let me introduce you to Pot."

"Oh, shut up. I'm not dealing with Bill right now."

"Somebody's scared." She said the words in the creepiest voice you could imagine.

"What about Candace's apartment? Is it far? I mean seriously, the appliances will be here tomorrow. They couldn't have come a day early?"

"My apartment isn't far. Why? Do you want me to go home?" She was standing outside the bathroom, dripping wet, and wearing a towel.

"No! I want to borrow your fridge. Would that be okay?"

"Yes. Give me a minute to put on some clothes."

She retreated into the bedroom.

"Somebody hurt that child badly."

"Yeah. She reacts like that all the time. I just hug her when she does it."

"Time. She'll come to trust us a little more."

"I know. But it breaks my heart when she does it."

"Just don't break hers."

"Never. I think this might actually be love."

"And don't forget you have something to tell her…"

"Oh, shit. I forgot. You suck."

"Payback's a bitch," I said with a cackle.

"And so's my roommate."

"*Touché.*"

Josie sighed. "You stay here, then. I'll run the blood to her apartment with her and talk on the way. Less awkward with you not around."

"Good girl." I packed all the blood up into a canvas grocery bag. Candace came out wearing her pajamas. "Aren't you going to be cold?"

"Flannel."

"Well, be careful. Thanks, Candace."

She walked over and hugged me, taking the bag and grabbing her fluffy coat.

"Good luck," I whispered to Josie.

She gave me the finger.

I locked the door behind the two of them and headed for my room. I planned on getting the bed warm for the two of them.

CHAPTER 7

My phone ringing was the last possible thing I wanted to hear. I reached over to the night stand and heard Candace squeak under the cover. I must have squished her.

"Sorry, sweetie."

I grabbed the phone and hit answer without looking at it.

"Hello?"

"Morning, beautiful…"

"What time is it?"

"Eight?" Jimmy answered.

"Jimmy, I'm very fond of you, but I literally went to bed two hours ago. Is this phone call a life and death situation?"

"Shit. Sorry, Dot. No, it's not. I was going to run up to Syracuse to take Mother to the airport. Just seeing if you wanted to tag along and hang out."

"If I had more than two hours sleep, I would be all over it like white on rice. Raincheck?"

"Sure thing."

"As a consolation I'll tell you what happened with Chief last night."

He chuckled softly. "I can't wait. Go to sleep."

"I'm halfway there."

"Hey, Dot?"

"Yeah?"

"Nevermind. Sweet dreams."

"Ima kill you." I pulled the phone away from my ear and stared at it. Wondering what he was going to say.

I slid the phone off and tossed it on the table, not giving a shit if the screen shattered or not. It didn't sound like it did, so I dozed off.

I woke up some time later and *really* had to pee. I lifted the cover off me. Josie had already gotten up, but Candace was buried in my side, arm thrown over me and her face pressed against my bare stomach. She had a bad habit of pressing her head on my bladder when she slept.

I ran my fingers softly through her hair, trying to wake her gently. She blinked and looked up at me. "I need to use the bathroom."

She nodded and flipped on her other side. I gave her my pillow and covered her back up once I slid off the end of the bed.

I tiptoed to the bathroom and relieved myself. I stared at the wall in front of me and wondered what time it actually was. It was almost unheard of to have Josie wake up before me. I hated to admit it, but I was normally somewhat of a morning person, even though Josie accused me of being an unholy demon.

The smell of brewing coffee drew me out of my reverie like the seductive hand of a lost lover. I finished, skipped brushing my teeth, and headed toward the kitchen.

"Morning, beautiful," Josie said jokingly.

"Bite me. I know I'm ugly in the morning."

"I figured you'd want a cup of crack."

"You're the bestest." I grabbed a mug and kissed Josie on the forehead.

"So. We're all still alive."

I'd actually forgotten about our guests. "You look relatively nibble-free. Think that one might be from Candace." I pointed at the hickey on her neck.

"Yeah. Since we had houseguests, we um… Nevermind. We used her apartment."

"Skank."

"Says the girl who anointed our living room."

"True. Did you tell her?"

Josie chuckled and grabbed the pot of coffee that had *finally* finished brewing. I needed to buy one of those industrial models that didn't give you time to scream obscenities at it. "Yeah. I told her what happened."

"I'm guessing she took it well if you got frisky, got a hickey, and came back home."

"You could say that."

"What did she say."

"That next time, she wants to watch, too."

"Dear Lady. What am I going to do with the two of you?"

She smiled over her coffee and wiggled her eyebrows at me.

"You're a perv."

"You betcha." She walked around the corner and sat on the stool, setting her coffee on the counter in front of her. "Who called this morning?"

"Jimmy. Wanted me to go with him to Syracuse to drop off the mother at the airport."

"You mention you were up late because of Mr. Bill and the Vlads?"

"You're a funny girl." I drank some coffee and leaned against the counter. "I told him about Bill."

"He likes it, doesn't he?"

I shouldn't have been surprised. Josie was as perverted as perverted came. I should have known she would have spotted his kink. "Yep. You should really consider going to school to be a therapist."

"You're not the first person who told me that. Maybe in a couple hundred years. We'll see."

I thought about it. In the 70s, I went and earned a degree in business management. Nothing else really piqued my interest. I wondered if I would find something else that interested me in the future… Maybe a vet or something. Who knew.

"So. When you gonna tell him?"

"Tell who what?"

"Chief about your guests."

"I'm not hiding it from him. I just didn't want to deal with it last night. In fact, I think I'm going to go check on the firehouse, have some breakfast, and stop by the police station."

"Okay. Well, I'm going to go snuggle with my Candy."

"Ew. It sounds creepy when you say that."

"You think everything that comes out of my mouth is creepy."

"True story. Don't get my sheets dirty."

"No promises."

I chuckled, not really caring. I did need to get in there to change, though. "Wait! Let me get some clothes. Oh, and listen for the delivery guys. No answering the door naked!"

I chugged my coffee, growled at her almost full cup, and got dressed. They were giggling under the covers when I walked out the door.

The drive into town was mostly quiet. Weekdays in Cedar Falls were. People either worked nights and were sleeping, or working during the day and off the streets. I smiled as I passed the diner. Food sounded really good, but I wanted to see how the store was coming first.

I pulled into the parking lot between my store and the police station. The dumpster was gone. I guessed they finished the demolition. A couple of work trucks were there, thankfully. I had given my one and only key to the contractors. It would suck not to be able to get into my own store.

Freddy Johnson was standing in the doorway looking at a set of prints.

"Hey, big guy. How's it going?"

"Well, we got her tore up pretty good. Upgrading the wiring now. Not much to look at, but go on in if you want."

I peeked in from the doorway. He wasn't joking. Walls were missing, wires were hanging, and rusted looking plumbing looked like a morbid skeleton winding through the structure. "Nah. I'm good. Gonna go get some breakfast. Have fun."

"You mean lunch? Breakfast was five hours ago. And I am having fun." He grinned at me as I turned around and headed toward the diner.

I walked slowly and nonchalantly past the plate glass window in the front of the police station and debated ignoring the knocking on the glass. Letting out a little sigh, I turned, acting surprised to see Chief standing there waving like a fool. I smiled and waved back, turning to head to the diner. He came strolling out the front door as I passed it.

"Mornin, Dot."

"Morning, Chief."

"Where you headed?"

I pointed at the diner. "Food."

"Mind if I tag along? I'm starving."

"Suit yourself."

He reached out and put a hand on my arm, slowing my pace. I looked up at him and he narrowed his eyes. "What did you do?"

I made a gasping noise. "What? Why are you assuming I did something? Can't a girl just go get some lunch without all the accusations? I mean jeez. I swear. What is wrong with this world. You don't see me accusing you of anything. Oh, by the way. The vampires showed up last night and are sleeping in my spare room. So yeah. If you want to get some food, let's go."

I pulled free of his arm and started walking. He lengthened his stride to match my pumping little legs. "The vampires. Are sleeping. At your house. And you're just mentioning this *now*?"

"Well, it was really late. I just woke up like thirty minutes ago."

"Dot!"

"Bill, they were wiped out. There's *two* of them left. They were bleeding on my doorstep. What was I supposed to do?"

"Call me?"

Lady damn it all to darkness. I hate *it when he makes sense.*

I sighed and backed my ass against the building, leaning against my hands. "I don't know if you know this about me or not, but I'm pretty stubborn, stupid, and self-reliant. I'm sorry. You're right. *Again*. It didn't even occur to me to call. I just… I would have told you once I got everything settled, but then I figured you'd just yell at me again."

He sighed. "I'm sorry, too. Yes, I might yell but it's only when you put yourself in danger. I wish you'd just realize it."

I opened my mouth to speak but couldn't. He *was* right. He did only yell at me when I risked myself. "You're worried about me." I smiled. It was nice to know how much he cared. Even if it did suck getting yelled at.

"Damn right, I am. If anything happened to you…"

I kissed him. Hard. Right there in the middle of fucking Main Street. Hell, I almost backed him *into* Main Street.

"Woah." He looked around, chest heaving.

"Worried somebody saw?"

He reached behind his head and scratched the back of his neck. "I… uh. Wow. Food?"

"Sure." I hid my grin. He was even cuter when he was flustered.

He followed me into the diner. I had a feeling I could have walked into the pits of hell and he would have followed me. He wasn't the only one, either. Jimmy, Josie, Candace, maybe even Dennis. I had good people. Our coven was coming together. I just needed to work on my relationships with Dwight and Jason. And David and

Connie, but they were in their own little world. They'd become the only married couple after the demise of the Connors.

"Hey, kids."

"Morning, Marge."

She looked at her watch. "Uh, been afternoon for a while, darlin'."

"Close enough. Can I get a coke and a burger?"

"Be right up. Usual, Chief?"

"Yep."

We sat down in my booth. I snickered. Chief hadn't even *tried* to drag me to the counter.

"What are you snickering at?"

"Oh, just your reaction to being kissed in public. Don't want your girlfriend to see?" I lied, but it was for a good cause.

"Yeah. The three of them are crazy."

"Four of us? Gigolo."

"Oh, you're including yourself in the ranks of girlfriendom, huh?"

"That's not even a word."

"Nice evasion."

"Thanky."

He sat there staring.

"What?"

He didn't answer, just gave me an evil smirk.

"Oh, you're not talking now, huh?"

No movement.

"You're really going to make me answer before you start talking?"

A single solitary curt nod graced his neck and the smirk broadened.

"Yes. I'm your damn girlfriend. Happy?"

"I am. But the other three might not be." His smirk turned into a full-blown grin.

"You are so dead." I started chuckling. "It's not nice to tease, especially since I *do* have multiple boyfriends."

"Good for you, honey," Marge said as she set our drinks down in front of us. I blushed several interesting shades of pink. I hadn't even heard her ninja-ass sliding up to the table. She hit me from behind. Chief looked like he was about to shoot kittens out of his nose, he wanted to laugh so hard.

She walked away without another word. My only fear is that half the town was going to think I was a slut by mid-afternoon.

"Oh, Lady. *That* was funny."

"Shut up." I wanted to crawl in a hole and die.

He did. And he got serious. "So, what is your plan?"

"Vampires or other?"

"Vampires."

"They're holed up for now. I healed them and fed the woman. Then Candace snagged a bunch of blood from the hospital, so they have snacks."

"You fed one of them?"

"Yeah. I didn't think she was going to make it."

He reached over and lifted my lip. "You look a little pale."

I slapped his hand away. "Shut up. I'm not turning into a vampire. You watch too many movies. I think. How do you become a vampire?"

"I have no idea. You'd have to ask them."

A little ball of fear curled up in my stomach. I needed to start looking before leaping. I forced myself to let it go. I didn't feel any different and I wasn't even wearing sunglasses. "Yeah. This is going to be fun integrating them into society. They've been off grid so long, they didn't even know what a shower was."

"Yummy."

"Yeah, but they don't stink, and they don't look dirty. Maybe they don't need to. Maybe that running water myth isn't."

"Isn't what?"

"A myth. Keep up. I wish I had a vampire expert to help."

"Um… Didn't you say you had vampires in Ashville?"

"Yeah, but it's not like they're…" I sighed. "I did mention I woke up thirty minutes ago, right? Let me call Mother."

He chuckled. Marge brought our food over and gave me a little wink. My life was over. I might as well invest in *Multiple Boyfriend's* T-shirts.

Chief bit into his burger while the phone rang. She finally picked up on the fourth ring. I swear the woman stared at her phone and watched it ring, just to answer it before voicemail picked up.

"Yes, my daughter? What have you done now?"

"Hello, Mother. I need a phone number."

"I believe it is 4-1-1, dear."

"You're funny, Mother. But, the number for information was disconnected many years ago. Live in the now, please."

"Shut up, ungrateful child. Whose number are you in need of?"

I braced for the impact. "The um… Abernathy's."

There was silence on the other end.

"Are you there, Mother?"

"Yes. Just trying to discern why you could possibly need the phone number of a clan of vampires, child. I'm not coming up with anything. Perhaps you could enlighten me?"

I sighed, not caring if she heard me or not. "Well, I may have picked up a very minute clan of vampires. Their clan was nearly wiped out by rogue witches hunting them…"

I felt her anger through the phone. "Be careful. They may come for the remnants."

"I thought so, I'll ward the house to high heaven this afternoon."

"Give me a chance to speak with Philippe. I will have him contact you as soon as night falls. You did well, child."

I blinked in surprise. Compliments from Mother did not come easy or cheap. It made them all the more special when they were received.

"Thank you, Mother."

The line clicked dead.

"What did she say?"

"She said I did the right thing?" All I could do was stare in shock at him.

"I hate to admit it, but you did. I just wish you had been more careful about it."

"Two compliments in the same day? And such a heartfelt one at that. Be still my heart."

"Shut up and eat your burger."

"Yes, sir, Mister Chief, sir." I saluted, too.

"Is she going to send help?"

"Philippe Abernathy is the head of the clan back home. She's going to contact him this evening and have him call me if he's willing to help."

"Good. Don't get bit before then."

"Har har. Funny man."

CHAPTER 8

"Can I talk to you?"

I had barely walked in the door. Josie was sitting on the couch, waiting for me to get home. Scenarios like that never ended well. "Um, yeah? Can I pee first?"

"It's nothing bad! Sorry, didn't mean to scare you."

"Yeah. Lead with that next time. I'll be right back."

"Wine?"

"Thought you said it wasn't bad?"

"It's not, but I'm trying to butter you up."

"This is going to be expensive," I said and headed to my bathroom, not giving her a chance to be offended.

I breathed a sigh of relief and finished up, washing my hands and reaching for a towel that wasn't hanging in its normal spot. I looked down and found it on the floor. I probably didn't want to know.

"Put a clean towel up if you're gonna use it to clean up your nasties."

"Sorry. I forgot."

I was kind of horrified that she didn't deny actually using my towel for nefarious purposes. I sat down on the couch next to her and put my back against the arm. "Next time I beat you."

"With a rubber hose?"

"Quit stalling. Talk."

"I–"

"Wait! Did the appliances come?"

"No."

"Damnit. Continue."

"I *really* like Candace."

"Yes."

"Yes?"

"Yes. She can move in with us. I like her, too. And I think it would do her some good. In fact, I was going to suggest it after we took care of our other house guests."

Josie stared at me incredulously.

"What?"

"You do realize you are turning into a mini-version of your mother, right?"

"I go out of my way to be nice and this is how you repay me? Insulting me to my face, you insolent witch?"

"Wench?"

"Whatever. Why do you say these things? Are you trying to hurt me?"

"Dot, I know she's your mother. And I know you see her in a certain way. You need to set that aside and realize your mom, while being scary as fuck, is astounding… And you're turning out to be just like her. Just a little more…rash."

I started crying. "Damn it, Josephine. Stop doing shit like this to me."

"Oh, honey," she said and got up and threw her arms around me. She started crying, too.

She finally let go of me and handed me one of the glasses of wine she had set on the table. I drank half of it and set it back down, wiping my eyes.

"You suck."

"You swallow."

"Ha. That' s a lie. Maybe once."

She snickered. "So how did Bill take the news?"

"That I swallowed?"

"Vampires. You're hilarious."

"Quite well. He even helped me come up with a plan."

"Yeah?"

"I called the Queen of Demons."

"And what did your mother say about it?"

"That I did good. She is also contacting Mr. Abernathy. He should be calling me this evening, hopefully with some aid or advice."

"No way."

"Yep."

"Shit. Chief's smarter than he looks."

"Be nice. Oh, and apparently, I'm his official girlfriend now. And if you hear anything around town about me being a slut… It was Marge."

"I can't even…"

"Yeah. It was an interesting afternoon."

The doorbell rang. I got up and, tired of surprises, peeped through the hole. There was a Depot delivery guy on the other side of the door.

"My appliances!" I flung open the door and scared the poor guy. "Sorry. A little excited. I haven't had a fridge in a week."

"I get that a lot. I'm hauling the old ones away?"

"Yes. Let me get some shit…stuff out of it. Them. Did I mention I'm a little excited?"

"I believe so. I'll start unloading the new ones. Okay if I set them on the drive until I get the old ones out?"

"You can put them wherever you want."

He gave me a look and shook his head. "I'll get to work."

"Slut," Josie whispered behind me.

"Today just isn't my day."

"Look at the bright side. You haz new 'pliances."

It only took him and the other guy in the truck an hour-and-a-half to get them in and set up. I was practically bouncing. "Can you get into Candace's apartment?"

"Yes?"

"Good. Let's go grab the blood. I want to have a meal for when our guests wake up."

"Aren't you little Miss Suzy Homewrecker."

I ignored her. "Do you think she'll mind?"

"I can text her, but I don't think so."

"Do. I don't want her to think we were being nosey."

"Okey dokey."

She wandered away to find her phone. Mine chose that moment to go off.

What do you want from Chinese?

"Josie, what do you want from the Chinese place?"

"We picking it up?"

"No, Jimmy."

"Shit. I was going to get something for Candace."

She came walking back into the room with her phone, fingers dancing over the keys.

"What do you guys want. I'll give Jimmy some money."

"Vegetable platter for her. Hunan beef for me."

"Okay."

I texted him the order and told him we'd be back in thirty. "Candace say okay?"

"Yep. With a smiley face."

"Let's go."

She lived closer than I imagined. We pulled into a guest spot and Josie led the way up the concrete flight of stairs to the second floor and unlocked the door. Cinnamon wafted over us as we stepped into the apartment. There was pink everywhere. I tried not to gag as I stepped into an Easter inspired nightmare. Pink bunnies, I was going to have nightmares for months.

"Wow."

"Yeah," Josie said with a giggle.

"I'll grab the blood."

"I'll rummage through her underwear drawer."

"And our conversation just sounded like an episode of Criminal Justice."

Josie laughed and stayed by the door. Thankfully she was joking about the underwear drawer. I opened the fridge and grabbed the bag of blood pouches. She had put the whole thing in there, and it was the only thing in there. "Doesn't she eat?"

"Why?"

"There is *nothing* in her fridge. Not even ketchup. How do you live without ketchup?"

"Beats me. Let's go. I feel guilty being here."

I closed the fridge and headed to the door. "Ready when you are."

"You get the feeling we're being watched?"

I turned around and looked. Not seeing anything, I tossed out a couple of tendrils of magic, just to test the waters. They were both zapped instantaneously and came crawling back to me pitifully. It hurt and must have showed on my face.

"You okay?"

"Yeah. Just got my magic scorched by something."

"Shield?"

"Or some kind of ward. Come on. She probably just has protections layered on everything."

"From what?"

"Who knows. I get the feeling she's running from *something*. She'll tell us when she's ready."

Josie nodded and pulled the door closed behind us, locking the deadbolt. "Strange."

"Yes, but she trusted you enough to give you a key. Look at the bright side."

"Let's get home. I haz the hungerz."

The sun was precariously close to the horizon when we pulled back into the driveway. Jimmy hadn't showed up yet. "Your stomach's going to have to chew on your backbone for a little bit more."

"Your boyfriend is late."

"It isn't even five-thirty yet."

We were unlocking our door when the truck rumbled to a stop behind us.

"Okay. I'll let him live."

I handed her the bag of blood. "Put that in the fridge for me, please?"

"Yep."

Jimmy *and* Dennis got out of the truck, Dennis laden with a large box of food and Jimmy with a twelve-pack. They looked like a beer commercial. Jimmy was handsome, as always. Rugged and sexy. Even Dennis, with his softer features, looked hot as hell. "Hey, sexies."

"Evening, beautiful," Jimmy said with a grin.

"Hi, Dot."

I kissed Jimmy and he headed inside. Dennis flashed me a smile. "Hey, handsome. What's shakin'?"

"Same shit, different day."

I laughed and held the door open for him. We all headed into the kitchen. Jimmy was putting the beer into the fridge. "Hey, nice appliances."

"Thanks."

"Um, Dot? Why is there a bag of type O-negative in your fridge…?"

I'd been so worried about telling Chief about the vampires, I forgot about Jimmy. "Um, we have a couple of houseguests…"

"Are they vampires?" He joked.

"Maybe."

"Wait, what? They're here?"

"Long story, but yes. The clan was attacked. Two survived. Amir and Yvette. They're in the guest room so don't open the door."

"Yeah. Don't worry. I won't." He stared at me wide-eyed.

"They're actually very nice. You'll meet them in a half-hour or so."

"The vegetable platter for Candace?" Dennis was pulling the food out of the box.

"Yeah." Josie snagged it from him and put it in the fridge, pulling out a couple of beers and handing me one. I popped the top and grabbed my dumplings and fried rice.

"Hey, Dot. Can I talk to you a minute?"

I set my food and beer down on the table and tried not to sigh. Desperately. I didn't want to have this conversation again. "Sure."

Dennis shot me an apologetic look as I walked past him, and I noticed Josie lingering in the kitchen, seeing if I needed backup. I gave her a gentle push toward the dining room.

"What's up?"

He wrapped his arms around me and gave me a gentle kiss. "Not going to tell you what you should and shouldn't do. You know I have your back. All I ask is you be careful."

I seriously debated throwing him on the counter and taking him right there. He couldn't have said anything more perfect at any moment than he did right then.

"I ever tell you how perfect you are?"

He blushed and started to pull away. I shoved him up against my new fridge and kissed the fuck out of him.

"Wow."

"Yeah," I said breathlessly. "You get story time later." I gave him a wink.

I grabbed his hand and dragged him to the table. Sitting down, I popped the lid on my dumplings and looked for chopsticks. Not, seeing any, I returned to the kitchen and checked the box the Chinese food came in. "Did they not give you guys chopsticks?"

"I don't think anybody in Cedar Falls knows how to use them," Dennis called back.

"Barbarians." I opened the silverware drawer and pulled out my set of good jade ones. I hated using them because the food had a tendency to slip out of them, but one did not simply eat dumplings with a fork.

As I was walking back from the kitchen, I saw Yvette peeking out from the hallway by the bedrooms. I waved her out. She seemed hesitant but stepped out into the brightly lit room.

"Everyone, this is Yvette. Yvette, this is Jimmy and Dennis."

Politely, they both stood and nodded at her. I could see her visibly relax. "Greetings," she called out softly. Amir stepping up behind her.

"We went and picked up the rest of your…food. It's in the fridge in the kitchen, if you're hungry."

Yvette looked ravenous. Amir simply nodded. They practically floated into the kitchen. I took a dumpling and dunked it in the little container of sauce, popping the whole thing in my mouth. They were pretty damn good.

"Dot?"

"Yeah?" I called back to Yvette.

"The large box or the smaller one under the counter?"

I smiled. "Be right back."

I headed into the kitchen and saw them standing in the center of the room, staring at everything. Instead of pointing, I opened the fridge and reached into the canvas bag, pulling out a baggie of blood. "They're right in here if you need more. Would you like it in a glass?"

They both nodded. "It was difficult drinking from the bag, but we managed." Yvette sounded apologetic.

I grabbed a pair of shears from the drawer and snipped the corner off before gently pouring the blood into two wine glasses. Having a flash of inspiration, I concentrated on the blood in the glasses and said, "*Bheith te.*" I handed one to each. "Come sit with us if you want. If the food bothers you, I understand."

Amir sniffed and took a sip, pleasantly surprised at the warmth I'd imbued it with. "Why?"

"Why what?" I asked.

"Why are you so accommodating for us?"

I looked to Yvette. She nodded, stressing his question.

I reached out and touched both their arms. "Because it costs nothing. You're safe. You have food. Welcome to Cedar Falls."

Not elaborating further, I headed back to the dining room and sat back down on my chair, tucking one leg beneath me. It took them a few minutes, but they both came in and sat at the remaining seats around the table. Yvette next to Josie and Amir next to Dennis, who nodded politely at his new seat mate. I covered my smile with a dumpling.

"Are you two husband and wife?" I tried making polite conversation. I could tell they were close.

"Amir is my brother."

"You both became vampires?"

"Not by choice, but yes," Amir added, calmly sipping his blood.

I sighed, not knowing what was polite conversation, and what was impolite. The last thing I wanted to do was offend either of them. "If I ask a question that is none of my business, I mean no offense and please tell me if I do so."

Yvette smiled and shook her head. "Do not worry. Please forgive us if our conversation skills are lacking. We are unused to speaking often."

"Well, we hope to remedy that. I hope you don't mind, but we're a chatty bunch."

Amir chuckled. Everybody at the table rubbed their arms. He covered his mouth and flashed everybody an apologetic look.

"Oh, my Lady. Could you do that again?" Leave it to Josie to like it.

Yvette started giggling. The looks on everybody's faces were priceless.

"I'm sorry about your clan, but I am very happy the two of you escaped."

They both looked at their blood morosely. "You have our thanks as well for saving us."

"The least I could do. I may have some good news. I hope you don't mind, but I sent a message to the clan of vampires back home… I asked for guidance to help you rebuild your lives here if you wish to stay."

Amir looked at me and I couldn't tell what he was feeling.

"Was that okay?"

"Again, I must ask why? Why would you go through all of this for two you just met?"

"You'll understand once you've known Dot for a little longer. It's her nature to help those in need. We were a broken coven, and she rolled into town like a tornado. Healed us and saved us all in the span of a week," Jimmy explained slowly and took another bite of food. "One question you never have to ask is what's in it for her. Helping others," he added thoughtfully.

I tried not to blush when Josie flashed me a proud smile. Between the two of them, I was going to start crying, again. Thankfully, my phone started ringing.

"Excuse me," I said and got up from the table.

I ran and picked up my phone, not recognizing the number, but the area code was Virginia. "Hello?"

"Young Dot?"

"Speaking."

"Greetings. This is Philippe."

"Mr. Abernathy! Thank you for calling and sorry to bother you."

"No worries. I spoke with your mother. She told me a little of what has transpired. Are the vampires still in your home?"

"Yes, sir."

"No need to be so formal. May I speak with the clan chief?"

"Certainly, one moment."

I covered the phone with my hand and leaned into the dining room. "Amir? Could you come here for a moment?"

He stood and strode gracefully to the kitchen. "Yes?"

"I'm speaking with Philippe Abernathy. He is the clan chief from the town I lived in. He wishes to speak with you. Is that okay?"

"On the…telephone?"

I nodded, smiling. "Yes." I handed him my phone.

He looked at it but didn't know how to work it. I gestured for it and put it in his hand and moved it up to his ear for him. "Hello?"

I patted him on the arm and headed back to finish my food. Yvette touched my arm gently and flashed me a smile as I passed by her.

"Ugh. I'm full," Josie said and pushed the rest of her food away from her. "Thanks for dinner, Jimmy."

"My pleasure."

"Let me give you some money. I know you weren't expecting to have to buy for the three of us."

"I'm sorry, but bite me," he said with a wink.

"Colloquialism?" Yvette asked.

"No. He really wants me to bite him. He's strange," I said and patted her hand.

"Dot!"

I laughed. "Just kidding, Yvette. Yes, it was a colloquialism."

She smiled and sipped her blood.

"So, what's new with you, Dennis? Haven't seen you in a while…"

"I've been picking up whatever extra shifts I can. My car needs a ton of work."

"Why don't you trade it in?"

"It's paid for. I'd hate to have a car payment."

I nodded. I thought about offering him my assistance, but he'd probably just get embarrassed and say no anyway.

"Dot?" Amir's voice echoed from the other room

I shoved the last of my dumpling in my mouth, vowing to save my rice for later. I knew I'd get hungry again. Chewing and swallowing, I slipped into the kitchen. He looked shocked and handed me the phone.

"Hello?"

"Greetings again, child."

"Hi, Mr. Abernathy."

"Philippe, please."

"What can I do for you?"

"I wanted your permission to send a pair of my clan to aid the lost ones."

"Lost ones?"

"Ones who have faded from society. Modern clans are often called upon to help them transition into the new era. They are an unmated pair. Two of our youngest. Would that be alright?"

"Of course. I thank you for your assistance."

"I also have a few favors to ask you in return. Do you have time to talk?'

"Sure. Hang on a second." I stepped into the living room and sat on the couch. "I'm set. What can I do for you?"

"I will be sending the two with the funds to purchase a home. Could you help them find a suitable location?"

"I'm confused. Is this a permanent move for them?"

"If they choose. I will leave it up to them. But even if they decide to return, I would like to have the house put in the clan chief's name. Would you be able to obtain documents for him as your mother procured for us?"

"I'm sure I can figure something out. But, if there is a chance that your clan is not going to stay, I would ask that you let me cover the expenses. The housing in the area is cheap."

"You would do this?"

"My pleasure. You know us, Philippe."

He chuckled softly. Surprisingly it didn't raise goosebumps on my flesh. It must only work in person. "The limitless resources of the Blackwells. I see it would be pointless to argue."

"Pretty much. Consider it an investment toward the town. This place is broken. I wish to see it thrive as Ashville does."

"Then take a word of warning to your adventure. Not everything went as well here as all would like to believe. Thankfully, your mother was able to align everyone to a common goal. Be careful."

"Wise advice. I will."

"I am planning on setting up business operations there as I have here, if you understand my meaning."

"Yes."

"Good. Could you gather some information for me?"

"I'll have the names of the corporation, and any board members, to you as soon as I can."

"You are a tribute to your mother."

"No, I am a consistent thorn in her side, but I thank you for the compliment."

"My clan shall arrive in two days time. You can keep them safe?"

"I have four witches in the house right now. We are about to have a warding party. If the rogue ones come for them, they will be safe."

"May the Night bless you, child."

"Lady's Light to you, Philippe."

I hung up the phone and called the diner.

"Cedar Falls Diner, Marge."

"Hey, Marge. Herb available?"

"Nope. He's married." She cackled. "Herb, it's Dot!"

I laughed and shook my head.

"Hey, Dot. What can I do you for?"

"A house. I need another house, Herb…"

CHAPTER 9

"This was as close to the outskirts of town as I could find."

"How big is it?"

Herb checked the sheet on his clipboard. "Four bedroom, two bath, a little over two thousand square feet."

"It's bigger than mine by a lot."

"Well, I figured for two of you…"

"Oh! Don't get me wrong. I love my house, but I've been getting a lot of guests lately and our permanent numbers may have grown to three. If it wasn't so far out of the way, I might have bought this one for us."

"Gotcha."

"How much?"

He glanced down again at the data sheet. "Sixty-three. A little pricey but it doesn't need a lot of work. The family that lived here took good care of it before they packed up and moved to Syracuse."

"Foreclosure?"

"No. They just couldn't ever sell it. Didn't want to take a hit to their credit."

"They're one of the lucky ones. I'll take it. This is a rush job."

"You want to see inside?"

"No need."

"Dot. Are you *sure* you don't want to see the inside of the house you are about to purchase?"

I sighed. I was being rash again and Herb was subtly letting me know. "Yes. I'll see the inside."

He nodded and looked like he wanted to pat me on the head. "So, any big plans for next week?" He found the right key on his gigantic key ring and unlocked the front door, swinging it open and letting me enter.

"What's next week?"

"Uh… Thanksgiving?"

"Holy shit. Is it really?" I stepped into a black and white nightmare. All the walls were white except one in every room had been painted black. The floors were checkered, the kitchen a jumbled miasma of black and white cupboards, countertops, and appliances. "Were they colorblind?"

"New York City folk who decided to move upstate."

"This hurts my eyes. I'll still take it, but I'll have to do something about the color scheme later."

I sighed. I had too much on my mind and too many things going on at once. My life had become a jumbled mess. I didn't know how my mother maintained her composure, and she had ten times my scale. Maybe I could at least delegate the new house renovations to Josie and Candace. Then again, maybe not. I don't think the vampires would appreciate living in a fuzzy pink house…

"Are you sure?"

"Yeah. I'll take it. The vampires will just have to deal with black and white until I can get back here to change the paint."

"I'm sorry… The what?"

"Vam–" I'd forgotten I was with Herb. A human. I sighed and collected my thoughts. He knew about witches, or at least we were a little bit different. He also knew not to ask questions. I'd just thrown around the V word without a second thought. I wouldn't be placing any bets on Herb's sleeping habits over the next few days. "Do you want the truth or to continue living in bliss?"

He set his clipboard down on the counter and sighed as he leaned against it. "I suppose the truth. It's not like I can unhear what you just said. Start with you and Bill. Aliens?"

"No. Witches. Real, honest to goodness witches. I'm a lot older than you, Herb. Bill is up there, but you're still his senior."

"So, witches, vampires, and werewolves are all real."

"You knew about the werewolves?"

"There were a few instances a while back of horribly mauled bodies. Chief said they were done by a wild animal, but the last body he brought in had bullets in it. Silver ones. I put two and two together, but just kept my mouth shut."

"Easier to sleep at night."

He nodded. "The vampires good people like you?"

"The best thing to remember about the supernatural community is they're just like people. There's good ones and bad ones. Never judge someone by *what* they are. Judge them for *who* they are."

"Yeah. Most humans can't get over different skin tones."

"True story."

"Thanks, Dot. For filling me in."

I nodded and put my hand on his arm, grateful he didn't flinch or pull away. "I'm working on it. Back home everybody in town knows about witches. Once we start turning the community around for the better, we'll come out."

"Be careful when you do. As I said, there are people who can't get past skin color, religion, or even politics. How do you think they'll react?"

It was food for thought. I'd been concentrating on what we could do, I'd been ignoring what we couldn't do. Even Mr. Abernathy had tried to warn me. Time was on my side, though. I could be patient and careful. I didn't need to transform Cedar Falls into a paradise overnight. I'd stick to doing what I could. "Wise words from a wise man. Thanks, Herb."

"Come on. Let's get out of here. I'll go get the paperwork drawn up and you can go give your bank another heart attack."

"They're used to it by now. Thanks again."

I hugged him and headed out to my car.

∞ ∞ ∞

"What are you doing right now?"

I chuckled at the seductive tone in Jimmy's voice. "Driving," I answered him through the Kia's Bluetooth. I knew what he wanted. We'd been too busy and had a house full of guests. We never got around to having story time last night. I knew he was disappointed, but he didn't say a word about it.

"Heading anywhere special?"

"Well, I was going to grab some lunch."

"Why don't you come over here. I can make tacos…"

"I like tacos."

"Good. Then get your pretty little butt over here."

"See you in ten."

The line clicked dead and my music started playing again. I sped up just a little, eager to spend some alone time with Jimmy. In a house not full of people and the undead.

True to my word, I pulled into his driveway ten minutes later. I hadn't even made it out of the car when the front door opened and he leaned against the frame, flashing me a toothy grin. He looked hot and I was very grateful I'd taken a shower before meeting up with Herb…

I got out of the car and walked up to the house. He held out his hands to be a gentleman and helped me up the three stone steps to his porch.

"Hey, handsome."

"Hi, beautiful. Got a kiss for me?"

I grabbed his hips and pulled him to me, sliding my hands up his back and devouring his mouth. "Mmm. Tacos."

98

"Yeah, I tasted them to make sure I wouldn't kill you."

"Bullshit. I know all firemen can cook."

"Never eat Dennis' food," he whispered. "Come on in."

"Is Dennis here?"

"Yeah. We both work tonight."

"Bummer."

We headed to their meager dining room. It was barely large enough to fit the small, round wooden table and four chairs. Everything had been laid out, leaving little room to eat. "You did all this in ten minutes?"

"I was cooking lunch for us and couldn't seem to get you out of my head. I took a chance you were done looking at the house."

"You chose wisely. I was going to hit McD's and head home all by my lonesome…"

"Beautiful lady like you should never be alone." The look he gave me told me he wasn't kidding.

"Neither should a sweet talker like you."

"Dennis, food! Go ahead and fill your plate."

I grabbed the one in front of me and grabbed a soft shell, piling it with fillings. "Smells delicious."

"Thanks."

"Hey, Dot," Dennis said when he saw me and plopped down at the small table.

"*Hola*."

He started making his, Jimmy beat him to the taco meat. "Too slow."

Dennis ignored him, used to his antics. I just enjoyed watching the two of them together. Everything was a contest and hilarity often ensued. We ate in relative silence, too busy chewing. "This is really good. Kudos to the chef. Oh, that reminds me, are you working Thanksgiving?"

"I am," Dennis said forlornly.

"I'm off."

"I'm sorry, Dennis. Jimmy, dinner is at four."

"I have plans…"

"What?"

"Kidding."

"You're a shit. Dennis, I *will* drop off a plate of food to you, though. Sorry you can't be there." I gave him a sad smile. He looked happy I'd asked, at least.

"Gonna be a big dinner?"

"Inviting the coven. Maybe my Mom, but I doubt she will come. Oh. Christmas… We're doing an early dinner and then I'm looking for volunteers to help at the diner. We're cooking food for those in need."

"I'm in. We both requested vacation that week," Dennis managed to say with a mouthful of taco.

"Really?"

Dennis nodded. "Kind of a tradition. Though I usually pull a shift if some of the married guys need off for their families.

"You're a sweet guy, Dennis."

He smiled and chewed, giving Jimmy a proud look. Jimmy rolled his eyes.

I finished my food and grabbed my plate, intent on taking it to the kitchen.

Jimmy frowned at me. "What are you doing?"

"Cleaning up?"

"You're a guest. And the rule in this house is guests don't clean up. I cooked, Dennis has dishes…"

"I'm not a guest."

"You are today. I have to be at work in three hours and I want to maximize my Dot time."

"Fine…" I laughed, still feeling guilty Dennis had to clean everything up by himself.

"Want to watch some TV?" He winked at me dramatically.

"I'd love to."

I followed him into his bedroom, smiling a little when I noticed how much he'd cleaned it since the last time I'd been there. It had been destroyed by Blake Connors since then, but he did a nice job of putting everything back together. It even smelled like pine trees.

"I bet you even washed the sheets…"

He chuckled. "I did."

"Why? We're just going to get them dirty," I said and kissed him, pulling him down on the bed. I almost scared myself with how much I wanted him. I hated to admit it, still uncomfortable with the enormity of my feelings, but it was all I could think about at lunch.

"How are you so hot?"

"Keep talking, Mr. Sweet Talker."

"No. I want to hear what happened with Chief."

I kissed him again, rolling on my side and laying my head on his chest. "So where do you want me to start?"

"From the restaurant," he answered huskily, wanting the whole story.

"Well, Chief was waiting for me when I got home. I kind of knew he would be. I could tell he was angry."

"Was he?"

"He thought you were showing off and doing it to make him mad. So, yes. But then after I explained why you did it he got incredibly hard."

"So, what did you do?"

Seeing the hunger in his eyes, I let my hand wander down to the front of his jogging pants. Slipping my hand over his already hardening cock, I lightly rubbed him through the material. "I lay back against the end of the couch, facing him, and let my skirt fall back. He was about three feet from me when I started playing with myself."

"Oh. That's fucking hot."

"It was until he had enough of watching me."

"What did he do?"

"Leaned across the couch and started licking me."

His cock surged in length under my hand. I lifted the waistband of his pants and freed it, wrapping my hand around it and continuing to stroke him. His velvety soft, hard flesh throbbed in my grip.

"Did it feel good?"

"It did. He has a very talented tongue. He fucked me with it."

Jimmy started breathing even harder, but managed to ask, "Did you come?"

"I did. Twice. His face was soaked."

"Oh, Goddess. You're going to make me come, too. What happened after?"

"His cock was trapped inside his jeans and it looked painful. I made him take them off. You should have seen it when it was free."

"Did you fuck him?" Jimmy's voice had a strange lilt to it, almost like he was afraid of my answer.

"No, Jimmy."

He breathed a sigh of relief.

"You don't want me to?"

"Yes! I do. But not before me. Is that weird?"

"Nothing about this conversation is normal, Jimmy. But I understand." I wasn't lying. I did understand how he was feeling. He didn't care if Chief slid his cock inside me, but he wanted to be there first. It was kind of sweet in a twisted way. I even agreed with him. I wanted Chief, but I wanted Jimmy first.

"So, what did you do then? Did you suck him?"

"No. I did something better."

"What?" He sounded desperate to know. His voice cracked in anticipation.

"I stood up and let my dress fall to the floor. I wasn't wearing a bra, but I had my panties on. I sat on Chief's legs and slid forward until his cock was pressed against my pussy. I used my hands to grind him against me while I jerked him off."

Jimmy groaned, unable to form words.

"And then I came again from grinding him against myself. And then he came. I almost came again when his hot come landed all over my chest, and then it slid down between us and dripped all over the front of my panties. It was so hot, Jimmy. I couldn't see, think, or move."

At the climax of my story, he came, spurting all over his shirt. Heavy wet stains littered the front of it as he convulsed and throbbed in my hand. I kept stroking, using his come as lubricant. He started shaking uncontrollably when I refused to relent. And yet, he never got soft.

"Please," he groaned.

"Stop?"

"No. Fuck me."

I almost shook my head, but stopped. Stopped to really think about it. I wanted him, there was no denying that. I also knew it was going to happen sooner rather than later. We were alone, with the exception of his roommate in the other room, and in a bed. I couldn't deny my need any more.

I let go of him, freeing myself from my leggings and tossing them on the floor. I kept my panties on, just to tease him a little, as I rolled over and on top of his legs. My shirt and bra were gone shortly after that as I sat in the same exact position as I had on Chief. Sliding forward, I pulled him to the crotch of my panties, the silky wetness of them rubbing against him. He pulled off his shirt and I ran my free hand across his sculpted chest.

"Is this what you were picturing while I told you my story?"

"Yes," he gasped.

I teased him like that for a few minutes before pulling my panties away from my wet pussy. I was literally dripping into the material below me. Gripping his hardness, I moved it around the thin material in my fingers and let go. He was trapped between me and my panties. I began slowly grinding my hips, pressing him against me and feeling him rub against my bare flesh. His hands gripped my thighs as I teasingly rode him, not giving him exactly what he craved.

"Dot…" He almost growled in frustration.

"Do you want inside me, Jimmy?"

"Yes."

"Do you want to feel how hot and wet I am right now?"

"Yes…"

I couldn't deny him anymore. Or myself. I didn't *want* him in me, I needed him. I lifted myself on my knees and moved the tip of him to the entrance and slowly lowered myself on him, gasping with each vein and ridge as he slowly pushed me open. I lifted up again, spreading my moisture around him and let myself fall on him, impaling myself. I cried out as he slid all the way in.

"Fuck, oh fuck," I muttered as I held myself there for a moment. Unable to handle anything else, I leaned forward and kissed him as I got used to feeling him inside me.

His hands slid from my thighs up to my ass as he pulled me into that kiss, sliding me forward on his throbbing shaft and sending bolts of pleasure everywhere in my body. I melted into him, moaning into his mouth as he lifted his hips and plunged back into me.

I pulled away. "Fuck yes. Are you going to fuck me like this or do you want me to ride you?"

He smiled and gripped my ass tighter, lifting his knees from the bed and slamming back into me. I had my answer. He spread his knees apart and found his rhythm, driving himself into me over and over. My moan became constant and rose in pitch. I lay my head next to his and buried my face in his neck as I continued vocalizing my pleasure. When it reached its peak, he pulled back until the tip barely remained inside me and thrust back in, triggering my mind shattering orgasm as he unloaded himself again, this time inside me. He pumped his hips a couple more times as he finished, letting go of my ass and wrapping his arms around me, holding me.

"What time do you have to be at work?"

"A couple of hours. Why?"

"Do that again," I whispered breathlessly.

CHAPTER 10

I unlocked my door and slipped inside, not seeing anyone alive or dead. I wasn't surprised about the dead ones, they had a couple of hours before they woke up for the night, but I was surprised not to see Josie lounging around.

A shower sounded heavenly. I wasn't going to lie, I was rather sore and sticky. I walked gingerly to my bedroom and found Josie reading a book in my bed.

"Hey."

She glanced up, took one look at me, and *knew*. She set down her book and gave me a shit eating grin. "I can't believe you did it! Finally!"

"How the hell do you know that?"

"Honey, if you saw your face and the way you are standing right now… You'd be asking how many times."

"Just twice."

"Which one?"

I sighed, dreamily. "Jimmy."

Her face fell a little. "Damnit."

"What?"

"I owe Candace five bucks."

"You were betting on me?"

"No. Just your sex life."

"That's kind of disturbing. And creepy."

"So's your sex life! Ooh. *Burn.*"

"Hahahaha. Good one. Get out of my room."

"I'm sorry, sweetie. I was just kidding."

"Fine, you can stay, but I'm taking a shower."

"Need some help?" She grinned at me.

"Ew. No."

"You're no fun."

"Remind me why you're my best friend again?"

"Charming personality and witty comebacks."

I gave her the finger and headed to the bathroom, tossing my phone and keys on the counter by the sink. I was halfway through the arduous task of taking my shirt off when the phone rang. I let it fall back down around me.

"What's up, Chief."

"I need you." His voice told me not to make any jokes about his phrasing.

"Where."

"Jason's."

"Oh, dear Lady, no."

"No. He's okay, but get down here."

I sighed and hung up, looking forlornly at my shower. "Soon, and you will be mine," I whispered and grabbed my keys. "I'll be back," I told Josie as I walked past her.

"Where you going?"

"See the chief."

She just chuckled.

It took twenty minutes to get out to Jason's trailer and I got lost twice. Chief had to flag me down as I was driving by before I saw it nestled in the woods.

Slamming on the brakes, I fishtailed to a stop, backed up, and turned in. I shut off the car and got out, almost frantically. "What happened?"

"I'll let him tell you."

I walked up the wooden steps to his trailer and pulled the door open without knocking. He was lying on the couch holding a cold beer to the large knot on his forehead. His shirt was sliced open, but luckily his flesh wasn't, and his jeans were charred from ankles to knees.

"What the hell happened?"

"Hey, Dot. Good to see you, too."

"Oh, sweetie. I'm sorry. Hello," I said as I crossed the distance between us, sitting down on the couch next to him. "Let me see." I reached over and pulled the bottle away from his forehead.

Gasping, I gently touched my fingertips to the lump, trying very hard not to put any pressure on it. Even the gentle contact caused him to wince. "*Leigheas,*" I canted, intent on healing the worst of it and letting the power flow freely from my hand. His face visibly relaxed after just a moment of work.

"Feel better?" I didn't stop pouring power into him even though I asked.

"Yeah. That's pretty amazing."

"Talk. Tell me what happened."

"I was having a quick nap before I had to go into work tonight, when I felt something hitting the wards Dwight helped me place on the property around the trailer. I went out to investigate and I find three witches I'd never seen before testing the defenses."

"What did they do when they saw you?"

"Kind of laughed and then they started bashing the wards with their power."

I had a sinking feeling I knew what they were looking for. "How did you get hurt?"

"I was pouring power back into the wards. That frustrated the hell out of them. They started to coordinate their attacks, two weakening the wards and one attacking me when she could manage to break through. Set fire to the ground around me once and then hit me in the head with a ball of force. The rips in my shirt were from a thorn wall. Luckily it was rooted, and I had room behind me to roll."

"I'm taking it they didn't get through," I said and finished the healing. He wasn't perfect, but the swelling had gone down immensely. I was getting better at it.

"No. I almost went down when the sphere hit me in the head but moved away from them to feed the wards. Luckily Bill showed up and scared 'em off."

"What did they look like?"

"Old. Not their faces or their bodies, more like they'd traveled through time. They were wearing beat up leather outfits and weren't speaking English."

"Did you recognize the language?"

"I don't know. It was very guttural, but not German. There weren't a lot of syllables."

That didn't help at all. "I'm glad you're safe."

"For now," Bill added from the kitchen, slowly sipping a beer and not looking happy at all.

"What?"

"Think they were looking for your new friends?"

"Actually, yes. Yes, I do."

"New friends?" Jason chimed in. "This have something to do with that vampire the other night?"

I nodded. "His entire clan but him and his sister were wiped out by these witches. They seem to be looking for them outside of town."

"Shit."

"Yeah."

"You need to get them out of your house, Dot."

I turned and gave Chief a withering glare. "I will not. I have reinforcements coming from Ashville to help them and bought them a house. But, until they're ready, they're staying right where they are. Where I can protect them."

"When are you going to realize not everything is your fight? When are you going to quit putting yourself, and the rest of us, in danger?" He barely got the words out through his anger.

He could have slapped me across the face, and it would have stung less. Jason must have sensed me tense, he put his hand on my arm. "Excuse me?"

"You heard me. They're vampires, Dot. They're not witches. They're not coven. Why is it up to *you* to protect them? You've ignored *everybody* when it comes to them. The minute he asked for help, you've been so focused on them, you stopped worrying about us."

I stood up, shrugging Jason's comforting hand off me. I didn't need to be comforted, I needed to be restrained. If one more word came out of Chief's mouth, he was going to need an ambulance. I tore my hate filled gaze from his pompous ass and looked down at Jason. One look, and I knew from his face, he was afraid of what was coming next.

"Could you please contact Dwight? I want you to check on him and then I would like the two of you in town until I can put an end to this mess. One way or another. Call me when you do get into town. I'll meet you at Farrell's motel and pay for your stay since all of this seems to be my fault, anyway." I paused to shoot Chief a scathing glare.

"Dot, would–"

I interrupted Chief with a hand. I held it up and looked at him, daring him with my eyes to say one more fucking word before turning back to Jason. "Could you do that for me? Please?"

"Yes, Lady."

"Thank you, Jason. I'm very sorry this happened, but you did awesome. And thank Dwight for me for his ward work."

"You're welcome, and I will."

I stood up and turned, taking a very long and deep breath, letting the oxygen clear my head. "The place looks awesome by the way. I don't even see a single beer bottle. Proud of you," I said, never taking my eyes off the slowly reddening chief of police blocking my way to the door. "Now if you'll both excuse me, I had just gotten home and was on my way into the shower."

I strode forward intently, not planning on stopping even if he didn't move out of my way. Luckily for him, he did, but he was also dumb enough to try to stop me from leaving by putting his hand on my arm and opening his mouth to talk.

"*Poll oscailte*," I shouted, holding my hand over the floor of the trailer beneath his feet. Shuddering the whole trailer, a hole formed beneath him, dropping him to the ground below, the floor of the trailer level with his chest.

Chief glared at her, clearly pissed. "Dot!"

"Sorry about that, Jason. I'll come and fix that later once you get the shit out of the hole."

His chuckle was music to my ears and helped drown out the shouts of Chief's obscenities as I walked past him and out the door, calmly getting into my vehicle and heading home.

My sobbing the entire ride home tarnished my victory.

CHAPTER 11

The great thing about showers is when you're standing under the water, nobody can tell you're crying…

It also didn't hurt that I was alone in my bathroom.

When the tears finally stopped, I shut the water off, holding the shower handle and staring at the white tile of the wall until the steam finally faded and the cool air made me uncomfortable.

Opening the sliding door, I grabbed the towel off the rack and rubbed its softness against my puffing eyes. I was glad I hadn't run into Josie when I got home, she would have known in an instant something had gone horribly wrong. I didn't want to talk about it.

I wiped the beads of water from my arms and shoulders before cocooning myself in my robe. Without any other thoughts, I wrapped the towel around my hair and crawled under the protective shielding of my comforter.

Let the monsters come.

I may have dozed off, I might not have. I was too exhausted emotionally to tell. For the first time since I'd left home, I debated the wisdom of coming to Cedar Falls.

It's not too late to tuck tail and go home.

But then I'd have to face my mother. And the goddess wants me here.

Are you sure?

Pretty sure?

It wasn't the first time I'd argued with myself, but it was the first time I didn't win. A soft knock on my door put an end to it. I even thought about asking who it was, but I didn't. I just lay there, letting my bed warm me and hold me.

The door opened anyway. It had to be Josie.

"I know you're awake."

"I know I didn't say come in."

"I know you wanted me to."

"No, Josie. I really didn't. If you could leave me alone for a few years, I'd appreciate it."

"Now I know you don't mean that."

She lay on the bed next to me on top of the covers and threw her arm over me, pressing her forehead into my exposed neck. "I know you don't want to talk about it."

"Well, at least you got something right."

"Yeah. I'm just here to comfort you and listen to you verbally abuse me. If that makes you feel better, go on ahead."

I rolled my head back until I could almost see her face. "I'm sorry. I know you're just trying to help. Forgive me?"

"Of course. I wasn't kidding. Whatever helps you feel better, that's what I'm here for. Just lay off the hair. I know it's not as pretty as yours."

"Oh, Josie." I flipped over and hugged her to me. "Please stop saying shit like that, you break my heart and I can't take any more."

"I was just making a joke trying to make you smile. Lighten up!"

"Berating yourself would never make me laugh. You should have said your taste in décor. Then I would have laughed."

"But I don't find your utter lack of chic decorating sense a laughing matter."

I chuckled as the tears started falling again. I remembered *exactly* why Josie was my best friend.

"How did you know?"

"Chief called and told me."

I snarled instead of cried.

"Easy, Tex. He knows he done fucked up. I guess Jason ripped him a new one for the better part of an hour before helping him out of the hole you threw under his feet. Impressive. Did you really call him a piece of shit?"

I nodded, not elaborating. "He's lucky I was worried about blowing the trailer apart. I would have blasted him all the way to Syracuse."

"So, not agreeing with him in any way, shape, or form, I have to ask. Were you so pissed off at him because there was an inkling of truth behind his words?"

"If he had talked to me and told me how he felt, I might have listened and thought about it. But you know Captain Arrogant-ass. He's got to be pissed off and snarky about it. Not to mention he did it in front of Jason."

"And you wonder why I like women."

"I'm just as bad as he is."

"But you have an excuse, I know your mother. At least you *admit* that you have a problem."

I pulled back from her a little. "Do you think I'm too focused on protecting strangers and not worried enough about my own coven?"

"If you had asked me before I met our houseguests, I would have nodded reluctantly. Now, I know you were right in doing so. They needed your protection and you had no idea Jason was going to get attacked. If you had, you would have got him out of that shitty trailer beforehand. So, no. You are doing just fine."

"The other vampires will be here tomorrow. I sign for their house in the morning. We're going to ward that house until it is a *fortress* and make sure they have lines of communication open to us at all times. I am personally going to find these rogue assholes and show them the errors of their ways and send them to the goddess for judgement if needed. That was my plan all along," I said angrily and determinedly.

113

Josie actually patted my head. "You do share some blame. You need to communicate your plans with those around you better. I knew. Jimmy caught some of it last night when he wasn't staring at you adoringly. But the chief of police and the alpha asshole of the coven, didn't have a clue."

"Yeah. If he wasn't so damn difficult to talk to half the time, I might have." I sounded defensive, even to my ears.

"Or if you weren't so busy staring at his dick and forgetting about everything else…"

"I'm going to pretend you didn't say that. Zorch marks on a white comforter are a bitch to get out."

She chuckled. "Our guests are up. I got them fed and sitting in front of the television, watching a movie. Do you need anything?"

"No. Leave me here to wallow in self-misery."

"Glass of wine?"

"And one of those."

"Be right back."

I pulled the towel off my head and let my hair flop on the pillow behind me, pulling the comforter over my head and hiding. The bottom of a wine glass nudged my hand. Without looking, I reached up and touched the hand holding the stem. It definitely wasn't Josie's. It was too rough and rugged.

If she let that asshole into my house, burning a hole in my comforter is going to be the least of her worries…

I let go of the hand and used it to peel the cover off my head slowly. I sighed in relief when Jason's concerned face came into view.

"Jason?"

"Yes, Lady."

"What are you doing here?"

"I did as you asked about Dwight, but I missed the beginning of my shift. Told the foreman I'd been in a minor accident and had an injury to my head. He gave me the night off. I was going to call, but I wanted to check on you in person."

"You didn't have to do that."

"I think you missed the part where I said I wanted to."

I smiled at him and took the offered glass of wine, taking a sip and setting it on the nightstand beside me. Sitting up, I propped the pillows behind me and scooted up, leaning against the headboard.

"Sorry about your trailer…"

He let out a short bark of laughter. "Totally worth it to see that."

I gave him a small sorry-not-sorry smile. "Yeah. I wish I could have seen his little feet dangling below the trailer. I should have crawled under there and taken some pictures. Heard you gave him an earful before helping him out."

Jason blushed. "Yeah. I feel as though I should explain something to you, so you understand him a little better. Can we sit and talk somewhere?"

"There's half a bed right here next to me. Park your butt."

"You don't mind?"

"Nope."

He walked around and sat against the headboard, tucking one leg under the other. "I think I should start with my sister…"

"Go ahead. I hardly know anything about her."

"I loved my sister dearly. She was sort of my personal hero when I was younger. As we got older, she was so much better at *everything* than me, I had to stop comparing myself to her or I would have gone insane. *One* thing she was never good at was making decisions. She was too carefree for that. She would wait until everything fell into place on its own and would deal with the aftermath or just sit back and smile when it did work out. It drove Chief nuts. It even drove me nuts. I don't think the rest of the Coven ever noticed or had a problem with it. Chief and I

115

used to roll our eyes a lot and then laugh about it to each other."

"Sounds like Josie."

Jason nodded slowly. "I can see that."

"So, what does this have to do with me?"

"The longer my sister was high priestess, the worse it got. If it didn't involve Bill or their own little world, she stopped caring. Bill kind of became the impromptu high priestess through her. He was the one who made the decisions and would guide her into thinking it was her idea. It was kind of brilliant and worked perfectly. Until she was murdered."

I didn't say anything. I reached out and put my hand on his leg. I knew it was still tough for him to talk about it.

"My point is this, Chief was used to running the show and I don't think he knows how to deal with you. You are the *complete* opposite of Becca in *everything*. Better. Her being high priestess made him into a know it all, and you inadvertently remind him every day that he doesn't know shit. It wasn't him who saved the coven, it wasn't him that caught the Connors, it wasn't him who turned us back into what we could be, it was *you*."

"You do know I didn't do that on purpose, right?"

"Absolutely. I just don't think he does. I'm not telling you to cut him some slack, especially when he's being a pompous boyscout with a superiority complex, but I'm telling you to remember *why* he might be doing things a certain way."

"You're pretty fucking smart. Anybody ever tell you that?"

"I watch and listen and learn. When you play second fiddle to someone for so long, it kind of becomes second nature."

I blinked in surprise. He wasn't just a pretty face, and trust me, it was. His sculpted cheek bones, icy eyes, and devilish smile would make anybody's heart flutter. But I wasn't sure if it was intelligence or wisdom. Rocket scientists could have problems tying their shoes. Sages knew it was easier to wear sandals.

"I'm going to keep you around just for your advice. I'm impressed."

He blushed again and it was almost too cute.

"Well, I should get going. Don't worry about the motel. I completely agree with you about staying in town, but I have some money saved. I can foot the bill. That's not fair to you and you know it."

"Bullshit." I got up off the bed, having lost all interest in wallowing in pity. "I meant what I said. This is my deal. Let me get dressed and we'll run you over there. I'll pay for Dwight's room, too."

"Well, just get one room with two beds. He and I can bunk."

"You sure?"

He nodded, not giving it a second thought.

"Okay, let me throw on some clothes." I dropped the robe without thinking about it and headed into my closet.

"Are you always this un-shy?"

"You've seen me naked already. Why would I be?" I grabbed a long-sleeved T-shirt and pulled it on before walking back out and grabbing a pair of panties and leggings, slipping them on under the top.

I turned quick enough to catch him staring at my ass. "Get a good look?"

His face turned crimson. "I–"

"I'm teasing."

He sighed and shook his head. I planned on having a lot of fun with him if he was going to be that easy to get flustered.

"Come on. Let's go."

∞ ∞ ∞

"Hi, Mr. Farrell."
"Hi, Dot. What can I do you for?"

117

"I'd like a room with two beds, not sure how long for."

"You came to the right place," he said with a chuckle and pulled the registry out from under the counter. I signed my name and put Jason and Dwight down as the occupants of the room. He closed the book without even looking at it, writing up the rental agreement on the standard form. Mr. Farrell was a firm believer in not using computers and printers. The motel didn't even have Wi-Fi. I wasn't even sure if he knew what it was.

I handed him my bank card for the deposit. He ran it through the clacking machine that imprinted it on carbon paper. "Just bill me when they check out."

"They?"

"Yes. My friend here and another guy are having their house renovated. I'm paying."

"Gotcha," he said with a wink.

I didn't even bother to explain further. Let him think what he wanted. "Thanks."

He took two room keys off the same hook and set them on the counter in front of me. "Let me know if you need anything else."

"I will. Thanks, Mr. Farrell."

He nodded and sat back down on his stool behind the counter, picking up his book and burying his nose.

I motioned to the door and Jason headed out. "Room two," I said and handed him the keys. He hopped into his rusted-out shit box and moved it over in front of his room. He grabbed his duffel bag out of the seat as I walked over.

"You all set?"

"Yep. Thanks, Dot. For everything."

"No. Thank you," I said, giving him a hug. He returned it awkwardly with one arm. "Oh. By the way, thanksgiving dinner at my house next week. Four o'clock. Tell Dwight."

"Are you sure?"

I nodded, giving him a little smile.

"Do you want to come in and have a beer? Or are you in a rush to get home? Sign says free HBO."

I almost said no. If I went home, I'd probably be under my comforter thinking about Chief, anyway. "Sure, but just one."

He tossed the bag into the room and opened Bessie's trunk, pulling out a worn blue cooler and carrying it inside.

"You come prepared."

"Wasn't sure if there was a mini-fridge."

"No. There's not. I'm surprised the units have electricity…"

Jason chuckled and nudged the door closed with his foot. He opened the cooler and pulled out a couple of beers, popping the top and handing me one.

"No chairs, either. Guess we're sharing a bed again," I teased, smiling at his blush.

I sat on the far side, laying on my side and tilting my head toward the TV.

He did the same and grabbed the remote.

He flipped it on but turned the volume down as low as it would go. Even so, you could hear muffled sounds buzzing through the speakers.

I took a sip of beer and let myself look at Jason. His forehead looked even better than earlier after I healed it. He barely had any swelling left and the redness had gone, too. "How's your head feeling?"

He reached up and absentmindedly rubbed the spot. "Pretty good. Can hardly feel it anymore."

I leaned in closer and got a better look. "You can hardly see it either." I let my lips close the last of the distance between them and gave him a gentle kiss over his vanishing wound.

He blinked in surprise. "What was that for?"

"Well, aren't you supposed to kiss booboos? That's what I always heard. I can take it back if you want."

"No. It's mine now. I'm keeping it." He gave me a little grin.

"Thanks for everything today. It meant a lot. Especially with Chief."

He nodded and turned the volume up on the TV a little. There was a movie playing and I had no idea what it was. At least it didn't have aliens. We finished our beers in relative silence, just enjoying each other's company. I set my empty on the nightstand but didn't feel like leaving quite yet.

"Want another?"

I shook my head. Between the wine earlier and the beer, I figured I shouldn't have another and then drive home. Chief would probably *love* to give me a DUI. I just watched the movie, feeling my lids getting heavier. I must have dozed off for longer than I had expected. The TV was off, and Jason had fallen asleep, too. I woke up with him laid out behind me, snoring softly in my ear and his arm wrapped around me. I blinked a couple of times and fought down the panic. We weren't doing anything, but it was very intimate. I could think of worse places to wake up. Namely Chief's bed.

I lightly ran my fingers over Jason's arm, trying to wake him. He snorted and reached up, cupping my breast gently. "If you're awake, I'm going to hurt you," I whispered softly.

There was no response.

"Jason," I said a little louder, softly elbowing him in the chest behind me.

"Huh?"

"Wake up. I need to go home."

He rolled over and started yawning. "What time is it?" He looked over at me, and I saw the hint of color on his cheeks as he stared at me wide-eyed, realizing we had fallen asleep together.

I reached into my pocket and pulled out my phone. "Almost one." I ignored the thirteen missed calls and texts. I could check them later.

"Dwight should be here soon."

"And I should get home. Call me tomorrow so I can check on you."

"Yes, Lady. I'll walk you out."

He got up and so did I, slipping my shoes back on and grabbing my jacket. He opened the door for me and I stopped before walking outside, giving him a small kiss on the cheek. "Thanks for everything."

"Thanks for the nicest night I've had in a very long time."

"Well, let me know when your next night off is. You can come hang out at my place."

"Is that a date?"

"Of course."

"Sounds perfect." He blushed again and I fought very hard not to give him another kiss. He really was too cute for his own damn good.

CHAPTER 12

Waking up in my own bed was much nicer, but a lot more crowded. Josie had been waiting for me when I got home. Half the missed calls and texts last night had been from her, the other half Chief. I didn't bother responding to him. Josie had been worried about me, reading me the riot act when I got home. We went to bed after I said goodnight to Amir and Yvette.

Sometime during the night, Candace had slipped into the bed with us and took her usual spot, arms wrapped around my waist. I was a little surprised that Josie didn't get jealous, but kept it to myself. She'd let me know if she was. Holding back was not one of her strong suits.

I tried vainly to slip out off the end of the bed without waking either of them up. Candace gave me a smile and a whispered, "Good morning," before scooting closer to Josie and snuggling up against her.

"Hi, sweetie. Go back to sleep."

I pulled on my robe and went out to the kitchen to fire up the coffee.

I breathed in the silence of the morning house. It had been a while since I was able to enjoy it. I didn't even growl at the maker as it brewed its magically caffeinated potion. I did snarl at the doorbell when it rang…

"Fuck me." I practically stomped to the door and flung it open.

"Got a minute?" Chief was standing there nervously, his left thumb hooked in his belt.

I debated slamming the door in his face. I also debated turning my front stoop into liquid cement, settling on stepping aside and letting him enter.

Probably best to get this over with.

"What can I do for you?" I kept my voice even and neutral.

He headed into the kitchen and grabbed two mugs out of the cupboard. My traitor of a coffee maker chose that exact moment to finish brewing and he grabbed the carafe, filling both mugs and handing me one.

"Thanks. Feel free to make yourself at home." So much for even and neutral.

He winced. "Sit?"

"I'm not a fucking dog. What do you want?"

He winced. "I deserved that."

"And so much more. Why are you here?" I walked over to the dining room table and pulled out a chair, sitting down and staring into my coffee.

"May I join you?" He at least said it politely.

I motioned to the seat across from me. "Just giving you a heads up, Chief. You don't get to do this."

"Do what?"

"Humiliate me, degrade me, and then come over the next day begging forgiveness. It… I don't work that way. I have never been more livid in my life as I was yesterday and I'm going to let you in on a little secret. I don't like to be angry. It makes me physically ill. So next time you want to tell me some bullshit story of how I'm putting strangers above our Coven, I will fry your sack and serve it for brunch with toast. Do you understand me?" I said my peace, evenly and without anger. Sometimes, I impressed myself

"Yes, Lady," he whispered.

"Good. Now get out."

Without a word, he got up and set his mug on the counter, heading for the front door. I almost stopped him. Only when the front door closed softly did I get up, dump my coffee in the sink and walk to Josie's room. I crawled into her bed and buried myself in her fluffy comforter, my tears staining her pillowcase. I was angry, and unsure if I could, or would, get over it. But I wasn't ready to let him go. Yet.

I lay there sobbing for a few minutes when I felt the comforter lift off me and Josie slide in behind me. Without a word, she slid one arm under me and one over me, pulling me into her embrace. I flipped over and buried my face into her chest, soaking her nightshirt instead of her pillowcase.

When I finally stopped, she spoke. "You did good."

"Yeah. He needed it, but that broke my heart. I doubt things will ever be normal between us again."

"They weren't so normal to begin with. He might be chief of police, but *you* are the high priestess of our coven. He needs to realize that, even if he doesn't agree with you."

I nodded, just wishing things hadn't come to a head at all. I was comfortable with our relationship and then he had to go be a dick. "Jason told me something interesting about Chief last night and why he is that way."

"What?"

I reiterated what he told me about his relationship with his wife and her effectiveness as high priestess.

"Makes you wonder why the Lady anointed her."

"Maybe because there wasn't anybody else."

"I guess."

"Let me out."

"Not if you're going to run after him."

"No. I need to pee, chug some coffee, and head to the bank and diner. I have a house to buy."

"Need me to do anything?"

"It's pretty clean, but we're expecting more guests tonight. Could you straighten up a bit?"

"Sure thing, boss."

"Don't start."

She slid out of the bed, letting me up. "Call me if there's anything else you want me to do."

"Help with warding later."

"The new house?"

I nodded. "Yeah. I want them shielded. I also need to get all the utilities turned on and install a phone at the house. I should have bought property in the center of town. I got it on the outskirts, thinking they'd enjoy the privacy, now I wonder if they're going to be safe. We could get to them in five minutes, but when you're under attack, that might as well be a lifetime."

"The wards should hold them off for that long. Jason did just fine."

"Jason is also a witch and was feeding power into them."

"So, they need a witch to move in with them is what you're saying."

"I wasn't, but I am now. You volunteering?"

"Oh, hell no. Not Candace either. Ask for volunteers? It's not like this is permanent. Just until the rogues give up, right?"

She'd followed me into the kitchen. I finally had another cup of coffee in my hand and *nobody* was going to ruin it. I took a sip and looked around the room, waiting for the doorbell to ring or my phone to go off. I sighed when I was met with blissful silence.

"I'm going to go get dressed and get out of here, before someone else tries to ruin my day."

"Good luck."

I took my mug into the bedroom, setting it on my dresser and pulling off my pajamas. I felt someone staring and turned to see Candace watching me, a curious look on her face. "What's wrong?"

"I wish I was built like you."

"Why?"

"You're tall, curvy, and beautiful."

I slipped on a pair of jeans, buttoning them up and pulling them down a little. They were a newer pair and still a little stiff. I almost put some leggings on, but I was going for warmth. I grabbed my bra out of the hamper and slipped it on, turning to Candace.

"You are beautiful enough. Any more and Josie might melt. She thinks you're perfect the way you are, and I do, too."

She blushed a little. At least the tiny bit of her face sticking out of the blanket did. "Thank you."

"You're welcome. By the way, are you working on Thanksgiving?"

She nodded.

"Damnit. I'll bring you a plate of food then. We're having dinner here."

"That's okay. I'm not that fond of turkey."

I gasped in horror and gave her a wink to let her know I was kidding. "I'll save you some stuffing, potatoes, and green bean casserole then."

"Thank you, Lady."

I walked into my closet and stuffed my feet in a pair of comfortable, fuzzy boots and grabbed a pullover hoodie to finish my outfit. The hoodie was warm enough I might be able to get away with not wearing a jacket. I doubted it, but one could hope.

"Alright. I'm off. Get some sleep, you. Don't want you passing out at work. Sorry I keep waking you up."

"I don't mind. I like talking to you."

I flashed her a smile, chugged my coffee, and headed off to face the world.

I called the diner and got the total for the cashier check I needed to bring and swung by the bank. They were getting less surprised seeing me there doing large transactions. The fun was wearing off. And after checking my available balance, I made a mental note to wire more money from my primary bank. I didn't want my bank card getting declined.

Check in hand, I walked into the Cedar Falls Diner feeling a little better about myself. Keeping busy helped. I waved at Marge taking a young family's order and waved the check at Herb. He nodded and didn't motion me back. I shrugged and sat in my booth. The reason he didn't wave me back became apparent when he walked out of the kitchen with a file folder, a pen, and a cup of coffee. He set all three of them down in front of me with a little smile. "Figured you'd be more comfortable out here."

"Thanks, Herb. You're the best."

"Hear that Marge? Ha! In your face."

I returned his small smile.

"You okay, Dot?"

"Better now," I said and sipped my coffee, determined not to think about Chief.

"Kay. If you need to talk…"

I nodded. "Thanks. This is for you." I handed over the check. He didn't even look at it.

"Everything is in there. Title, too. I'll grab the keys out of the safe."

"Thanks."

"Know what you want to eat?"

"Know what? Surprise me, Herb. I'll have the special."

"We don't have a special."

"That's why I said surprise me."

He chuckled and waddled back to the kitchen. Marge swung by and dropped off my usual coke, too. I sat there sipping my coffee while I signed the paperwork and looked through the file. I was *almost* disappointed Herb didn't let me use his office. I would have been free to use my magic to speed the process along. I'd been reduced to using my hand like some sort of barbarian. I took my time, lazily making the loops in my name as I signed.

The chime over the door went off and I didn't look over. I knew who it was. I could almost feel him slither through the open door. That, and I smelled his aftershave. I knew I was still pissed at him when it didn't induce happy feelings. Instead, the smell kind of made me nauseous.

"Lady," he said softly as he walked past and headed toward the counter, sitting on one of the stools. Marge shot him an unusual look and then turned her gaze to me. I pretended not to notice.

"What you do now?" She asked him loudly enough that the entire restaurant heard her, putting her fist on her hip.

I watched for his reaction. He shook his head at her and picked up a menu.

"Now I know you screwed up. You haven't looked at a menu in ten years." She grabbed a rag and moved away to clean a vacated table.

I went back to signing but saw him cast a nervous glance over his shoulder in my direction. It was almost fun watching him squirm.

Marge moved on to another table and another, finally cleaning the booth next to mine. "Food should be right out, darlin'. Need a refill on the coffee?"

"No, maybe after lunch."

"What did he do?" She whispered the question, but I'm pretty sure everybody could still hear her. A couple of tables' giggles told me I was right.

"I don't know who you're talking about." I never looked up from the inspection sheet I was signing off on.

"Oooh. Musta been bad." She shuffled off and I couldn't help but laugh when she slapped him in the back of the head with the dirty rag.

He rubbed the back of his head and wiped it on his pants, finally turning around on his stool and giving me a pleading look. I reached down, picked up my coffee and took a sip, staring into his eyes the whole time. I set the mug back down and turned my attention back on the paperwork.

I finally finished, almost sad I didn't have the distraction anymore. It would make ignoring people that much more difficult. Luckily, Marge delivered my food. I gave myself a mental fist bump.

"That looks delicious. What is it?" She turned the plate as she stared at it.

I'm guessing if Marge didn't know, it wasn't on the menu. "I don't know. I told your husband to surprise me."

"Oh, goodness. I'll go get you the Pepto from the back. Keep some in my locker."

I laughed as she wandered off. Hopefully not returning with a pink bottle. Whatever Herb had made me, it was deep fried. I broke it in half and gasped a little. "No way."

I carefully bit into the corner. It exploded on my tongue and I could taste each individual flavor as I chewed, but they blended together perfectly. It was like lunch and dessert in one meal. Herb, that culinary diner genius, put peanut butter on one slice of bread, hazelnut spread on another, and then squished banana between them, dipped the whole fucking thing in batter, fried it, and covered it in powdered sugar…

I could feel my arteries clogging and my endorphins dancing. I couldn't have asked for a better pick me up after the couple of days I'd had.

I must have groaned a little. Or a lot. Everybody in the restaurant had turned to watch me eat. "Sowwy," I managed to choke out with a mouthful of heaven.

"Is it too late to change my order?" One of two girls sitting at the square-top table asked Marge.

"Since I don't know what it is, you can't."

The girl looked crestfallen.

"It's our new sandwich. It's called the Dot," Herb yelled through the window. "It's a super-secret new menu item, only for those in the know. I'll swap out your order. You had the burger no mustard?"

The girl nodded, nearly bouncing in her seat.

I munched on a fry, trying not to blush and failing miserably. To have a sandwich named after you at the local diner was the highest order possible bestowed upon anyone. I might have to change my name to Lady Dot. Lady Dorothea was a little too prissy.

Instead of looking over at Chief, I gazed out the window as I ate, taking in the sights of people wandering Main Street. I wished with all my heart that the bookstore would open soon. I knew it wouldn't be until after the new year and it left me a little melancholy. I would have loved to have decorated the store for Yule.

There's always next year. And the next few centuries after that.

I tried to picture the city street the way I wanted it to look. The ultimate end of my goal. A bustling little rural metropolis of happiness. There were some meager decorations on the light poles already, and a few strands of lights strung up in the couple of businesses that had survived the plight of the economy crashing. I wanted more stores, more lights, and pine garland galore. Somebody needed to wrap the light poles with red ribbon, too.

It will happen. This mess has just made me more determined.

Fuck Chief.

That thought let in little images I did *not* want to be picturing.

Marge set another plate of food on the table on the other side of the booth and walked back behind the counter. "Food's up," she told Chief and pointed at my table.

I'm going to turn her into a bat.

Chief honestly looked afraid. "Marge," he hissed.

"It's fine," I said loud enough for him to hear. Ignoring him, I concentrated on my sandwich. I wanted to eat it as quickly as possible before it cooled. At least that's what I told myself.

I heard his sigh and his stool swivel as he turned around.

"Don't expect a tip." I knew he was glaring at the busy-body behind the counter. I could feel the heat from it.

131

"Here's a tip for *you*. Stop being an ass and tell her you suffered one too many head injuries."

Everyone in the restaurant laughed, until Chief looked around at all of them, memorizing their faces. I could even mentally picture him pre-writing their names in his ticket book.

"I need to call the network. There's enough drama from the two of them for twelve new shows."

"Order up," Herb said *loudly* to his wife.

"Yeah, yeah. I kinda wanna see how this plays out," she told him.

I wanted to crawl in a hole. With my sandwich, though.

Chief set his coke down on the table by his double burger and fries. "I'm sorry for this," he whispered as he slid in.

"I know." I took another bite, overstuffing my already full mouth.

"So, what's in the Dot?"

I sighed with a mouthful of food, chewing quickly and swallowing. "Little bit of rage. Lotta bit of regret. And a smidgeon of sorrow."

"That's some weird ingredients for a sammich."

"Oh, you meant the sandwich. Sorry. That's hazelnut spread, peanut butter, bananas, deep fried to golden perfection and sprinkled with powdered sugar. Or crack. Maybe both, I might be addicted."

Absentmindedly, I picked up my untouched half and offered him a bite.

Surprisingly, he leaned forward and tried it.

"Holy shit, that's sweet."

"That's why he named it after me."

He burst out laughing, trying to cover his mouth and saving me from the spray. I handed him a napkin and he wiped his hand and mouth, still chewing and laughing. I didn't know whether to be offended or not. I decided to go with not. I grinned at him.

"That tastes really good, though."

132

I leaned forward and looked around. I whispered, "That's the other reason he named it after me."

I'd managed to wait until he was taking a sip of his coke. This time there was no saving me from the spray. He looked like a breaching whale. I thought I might have seen a rainbow for a moment.

I sat there staring at him in disbelief, coke mist slowly coalescing into drops and running down my face. He didn't know if he should run or laugh more.

"I am *so* sorry. Oh, my Lady." He got up and ran to the counter. "Can I have a clean towel?"

"Smooth move, ex-lax," Marge said and handed him a clean, folded dishtowel from behind the counter.

He ran back over, offering it to me.

I chuckled as I took it from him. "Okay. That one was my fault."

He sighed in relief and sat back down. "I can't believe you said that."

"Sort of just popped out."

"Yeah, but now I'm trying to picture how Herb knows how you taste. I'm not feeling well."

I gasped and turned green. I'd missed that little bit of logic with my witty remark. We both looked up at each other at the same moment wearing the same expression. It was a good thing both of our mouths were empty. We lay back in the booth laughing together.

"See, isn't this better?" Marge started wiping drying coke off our table and putting down a stack of fresh napkins. "I'm kind of a genius sometimes. I scare myself."

"And Herb," Chief added, much to her dismay.

"Careful, Chief. I serve your food." She turned and walked away.

He sighed. "I just seem to piss all the women off in my life."

"Well, you can be an asshole sometimes."

"Sometimes?"

"Every once in a while, you're kinda sweet." I was being honest when I said it. "You're lucky you have a great ass."

He smiled at that and sat back up. He picked up his burger but didn't' take a bite. "I do owe you the biggest apology in the history of saying I'm sorry. I was way out of line yesterday, Dot. I hope you can forgive me. One day."

"Eat. I forgive you. Don't do it again."

"I won't. Or at least I'll try really hard not to. I promise."

"I may stab you next time. Let that be a deterrent."

"Don't need to. The look you gave me was deterrent enough."

I nodded. I could only imagine what I looked like.

"I had a long talk with Jason last night. He told me what it was like when Rebecca was high priestess. I didn't know. I'm sorry."

"It wasn't bad, just frustrating at times. I had all the responsibility and I got used to it. Then you came along, headstrong and adamant. It may take me a while to get used to that."

"But you still want to?"

"Want to what?"

"Get used to it," I said nervously, afraid to hear his answer. I wasn't lying to myself when I said I didn't want to end it. I was just worried he might…

"Very much so."

"Okay." I breathed a quiet sigh of relief.

He nodded, taking another bite of burger and shoving a french-fry in his mouth. I started nibbling on the other half of my food.

"What about *us*."

"I haven't forgiven you *that* much. Give me time to cool down. I'm still pretty pissed."

He nodded. "I understand and deserve it."

At least he understands. I may not want to end *our relationship, but that doesn't mean everything is going to be shits and giggles right off the bat.*

"Not to start an argument, were you just pissed and trying to make me angry, or did you really think I was putting them before the coven?"

"I thought about it all night. I don't trust them like you do. Call it what you want, but they are what they are. However, with that said, what I should have yelled was that you were putting them before what *I* wanted. It didn't have anything to do with the coven. You weren't doing what I wanted and that freaked the fuck out of me and I'm disgusted by myself. Too used to getting my way."

He really was disgusted with himself. He pushed his food away. I could tell it took a lot of soul searching and everything he had to tell me that.

"Thank you for being honest."

"Thank you for making me be honest with myself."

I nodded. Anger was still swirling in me, but it had died down from a category five hurricane to a tropical storm. Hopefully the low-pressure system would move off the coast and we'd have clear skies ahead.

I tossed him an olive branch. I reached across the table and stroked his hand with my fingers. He didn't try to hold my hand, but he turned his palm up, offering me his. I set the check for lunch in it and gave him a grin.

He chuckled. "My pleasure."

"I was teasing. Give it back."

"No. It's the least I could do."

"No. The least you can do is come help me ward the new house I bought for our friends."

"The ones staying in your current house?"

I nodded.

"I like this plan."

"I figured you would. With the two coming tonight, there should be plenty of room for them. And they'll be on the outskirts of town. Giving them a bat-phone to get ahold of me in emergencies." I had a flash of brilliance. "I might need to get ahold of my mother, though."

"Why?"

"If they call for backup, it will take a minimum of five minutes to get there. We could shield and ward the shit out of that place but without someone on the inside to maintain the wards, the rogues will wear them down quickly. I want a volunteer to stay with them to *be* the battery."

"And you don't want to risk any of our people."

"No. It's not that. I don't want anyone to *think* I'm risking our people. Does that make sense?"

"You mean me…"

"Not just you. But, yes. You are included in that."

"Fair enough."

CHAPTER 13

We picked up Josie and Candace on the way. She had a few hours until she had to be at work and volunteered her services. Josie didn't look surprised when I showed up with Chief.

We headed toward the house, the girls in my SUV and Chief in his Jeep behind us. I got lost on the way and had to plug the address from my paperwork into my mundane GPS.

Josie finally got around to asking. "So, you forgave him, huh?"

I nodded. I really didn't want to talk about it, she was smug enough. "Mostly. I'm still pissed, but I no longer want to send his man bits to a taxidermist."

To stop the conversation from progressing further, I called my mother. For once in her life, she was the lesser of two evils.

"Hello, favorite daughter," she answered, her voice echoing over the car speakers.

"Hello, second favorite mother." Two could play that game.

"You amuse me to no end. What to you require now? Did you pick up a litter of lycanthropes?"

Candace was having giggle fits in the back seat. Josie shook her head at her, wide-eyed, making shushing faces.

"Who is that charming creature with the melodic laugh?"

"Candace, one of ours."

"Next visit, you shall have to introduce me to the rest of yours."

"You'll see them at Yule, Mother. You are still coming?"

"Perhaps the day after. Festivities shall be in full swing here."

"Meaning you'll be skyclad in a house full of hand-picked male members."

"Perhaps."

I sighed, fervently trying not to picture that. "I did call for a favor, though."

"I'm shocked. Usually you call just to chat."

The sarcasm is strong with this one today.

"I need a witch."

"You have some."

"I need more."

"Why?"

She doesn't beat around the bush. Maybe she does, but I don't want to picture that either…

"My protection offer to our new vampires has come with some…differs of opinion on the matter within the coven. I have established a sanctuary for them and the ones being sent by Mr. Abernathy. We're on our way to ward the place now, *but* one of our witches was attacked by the band of rogues. He's okay, but fought hard to maintain the wards against them. I need someone who is willing to share space with vampires and maintain the wards long enough for the cavalry to arrive…"

"And the Coven of the Black Well is used to vampires."

"Yes."

"This is just until the rogues move on or are destroyed? Or is this a recruitment offer, as well?"

"I won't lie. That is not my intent but would be welcome. If someone is willing to relocate with a more permanent intention… I would not say no. Our numbers are few."

"How many?"

"In our coven? We are down to ten."

"That's hardly a coven, but I was referring to recruits. Some are restless and news of your pioneer efforts and deeds are spreading like an infection. You might get more than you could handle."

That kind of surprised me. I loved Ashville. If it weren't for the goddess induced itch driving me away, I'd never have left. "You'd be surprised what I can handle, Mother."

"That sounded dirty, daughter. I shall put the word out as well as your phone number. You can interview and pick and choose for yourself. I won't let half the coven relocate, though."

"Fair enough. I thank you for your gracious offer, Mother."

The line clicked dead without a goodbye. I was still in shock. Josie looked almost apoplectic. "How the hell do you do that?"

"What?"

"Snap your fingers and get an army."

"A few witches is hardly an army."

"She was scary," Candace's voice peeped from the back seat.

"You don't know how right you are, baby. If Dot's not around, and you see her, run."

"Don't scare her! She's not that bad. Most of the time."

We pulled up to the new house. "Chief and I will be on warding duty. You two handle the house. No pink."

"What do you mean?"

"You'll see."

We got out of the car, waited for Chief, and I unlocked the door, pushing it out of the way so they could see the monstrosity I had bought.

"Why did you buy an art museum?" Chief made a face as he looked around the interior.

"That's putting it generously. Looked like a mortuary to me," I answered Chief.

"I don't understand. What's wrong with it?" Josie asked, confusedly.

Maybe I shouldn't have put her on redecorating detail.

Chief and I left them to it and created a perimeter ward around the edge of the property, using magic to create a hedgerow worthy of holding the spell. Windows were salted, protections cast, and we even put in a few traps and power sinks. By the time we were done I was exhausted but satisfied.

"You might not need that internal power supply…"

I looked up at Chief. It was cold out, but I was nearly out of breath and sweating. It had been almost pleasurable casting the wards with him. Our magic was very…compatible, for a lack of a better word. If they weren't, casting the spells would have been twice as hard and worked only half as well.

"Well, better safe than sorry. I called my mom on the way."

"How'd that go?"

"She's putting the offer out to the younger members of the coven. Especially to those who might consider making the move a little more permanent. We might be getting a few more members to our little coven."

"I don't know how to feel about that," he said thoughtfully.

"Bigger isn't always better, but we're in a position to hand pick who stays. Mother is setting up some phone interviews, but… I would like you to be with me when I do the personal ones. I'd like your input. How's that for fucking compromising?" I smiled to let him know I was teasing.

"I'm impressed. And I thank you."

My smile got a little bigger. If he was willing to work with me, I could return the favor.

"Hey," he said.

"What?"

"Think your mother might be sending someone to spy on you?"

I laughed. I hadn't thought of it, but it was more than likely. "Probably."

"That doesn't make you mad?"

"No. I would expect nothing less."

"You and your mother ever go to therapy?"

"Once, and then she slept with him and he told me I was an awful person."

"Are you kidding me?"

"Yep."

"Dot?"

"Yes."

"I missed you," he said happily.

I nodded. "You do have entertainment value. I've had to take up knitting. *Knitting*, Bill."

He chuckled in the cool afternoon air. "Dot?"

"Yes?"

"Would you mind if I hugged you?"

I thought about it. Not going to lie, I really wanted that hug. "Okay, but no kissing."

He took the step forward, slipping his arms through the jacket I'd unzipped because I was hot. His arms wrapped around my back and pulled me close to him. My head settled instinctively against his chest.

"Didn't say you could feel me up, either."

"Are you complaining?"

"No."

His chest vibrated as he chuckled.

"Look at me," he whispered.

"No. I'm afraid."

"Of what?"

"Not being mad at you anymore."

"Would that be so bad?"

"No." I lifted my head.

His head lowered and I lifted myself on my toes, my lips meeting his halfway. My hands found his face, pulling him to me harder.

Anger is an overrated emotion, anyway.

My lips parted, and his tongue slipped into my mouth, intertwining with mine. We both whimpered as we let the kiss grow into something desperate, his hands sliding down onto my ass and then back up under my hoodie, cooling my skin but making me hotter.

I pulled back. Not because I wanted to stop, either. I just didn't want it to progress to a point where we wouldn't be able to stop. Not the best idea standing outside a house in the snow.

"Wow. I missed kissing you." He pulled me a little tighter, but just for a moment.

"It's only been a little over a day. Jeez, you addict."

"To you?" He cocked an eyebrow. "Bet your ass."

"That's a big bet."

"Your ass isn't big, it's perfect."

"Bet you say that to all the high priestesses you want to have makeup sex with."

"I can honestly say that is a true statement."

I laughed, but silently hoped he meant me and not Rebecca, too. I wasn't jealous. Nope.

"Shall we go see what color they made the walls?" He laughed and motioned to the door.

"Hold me. I'm afraid."

"Awww, shucks. Okaaay."

I closed my eyes as we opened the front door. It quickly turned into a sigh of relief. They'd gone with neutral creams and light colors. I did a little fist pump as I walked through the house, not seeing any pink. Until we got to the last bedroom, opened the door, and saw Josie lying on top of Candace, kissing her deeply.

I covered Chief's eyes. "Knock it off, you two."

"Oh, you can kiss and we can't?"

I stared at Josie in shock but then walked over to the window. Sure enough, it overlooked where we had been standing, lip-locked. "You little perv."

They stood up, Josie pointed at Candace. "It was her! She practically attacked me after watching you."

I was opening my mouth to call her a liar when Candace blushed and looked at the floor. She hadn't been lying. Chief started chuckling and walked back out into the living room, not wanting to get into the middle of it.

I sighed and followed him, rubbing the top of Candace's head as I passed her. It wasn't as if I could yell at *her*. She might start crying.

"We better get home. We're going to have guests soon."

∞ ∞ ∞

It was getting late when the doorbell rang. Amir and Yvette had lifted their heads from the movie they were watching a moment before it sounded. I should have known someone was here. They glanced at each other nervously.

"I'll get it."

I opened the door and my jaw almost hit the floor. I'd seen some of the vampires in Ashville. Most of them were older, not that you could tell from looking at them, more from the feeling of power that washed over you when you stood too close. They dressed elegantly, not trying to hide what they were. But that was Ashville, and not the pair standing on my porch.

The girl looked eighteen. She was obviously of Japanese descent. Her face was beautiful, and her mouth drawn up in a mischievous smile. Her lips were purple and matched her hair, the half that remained on her head. The other half had been shaven down to her skull. Earrings ran from her lobe, wrapping around the outer edge and some even dangled from the cartilage inside. Her bottom lip was pierced twice, the hoops looking like bottom fangs. Her eyebrows had lines shaved vertically through them and she was covered in tattoos. Wearing no jacket and not shivering in the least, she wore her tube-top, overalls, and sneakers with pride.

He looked just as young, but only half-Asian. His hair stood up on end, spiked and dyed blue. He wore a chain adorned black leather jacket over a gaming console T-shirt, and skin-tight black leggings with leather boots. They were adorable. I wanted five more. I wondered if Mr. Abernathy would let me keep them.

Both were showing fang as they smiled.

"Hi, I'm Dot. I'm assuming Mr. Abernathy sent you?"

"I'm Yuki and this is George. Yes, he did. Heard you inherited some vampires?"

I nodded. "Amir and Yvette. Lost ones, I think he called them. Come on in," I said. They both nodded, accepting my invitation before crossing the threshold. I wondered what would happen if they tried without one.

They huddled together as they walked into the house. Amir and Yvette stood and bowed low. "Greetings," they said in unison.

"Woah. Way too formal. We're here to get you into this century. But, hi!" George's voice was like three octaves lower than I was expecting.

"Well, I'm sure you four have a ton to talk about. I've secured a home for the four of you and it's warded all to hell." I turned to George and Yuki. "But one of our witches was attacked by the rogues yesterday. We're not ready to move you in, *yet.* You'll be safer here. We're going to have a witch stay with you until the rogues leave or are dealt with, if that's okay?"

Yuki shrugged and George nodded.

"Trouble finding a volunteer?"

"Our coven is *tiny.* I've called my mother for some reinforcements. I'm hoping they'll be here within the next few days."

"You are Madeline Blackwell's daughter?"

I nodded at Yuki. She backed up a step involuntarily.

I was used to it.

"It's okay. I'm a little more normal."

George elbowed her in the ribs. "Smooth."

I chuckled. "Can I get you guys something to drink? I have wine, beer, and a little blood left." That reminded me. I had some work to do for Mr. Abernathy. I really didn't want Candace getting busted at work for stealing blood. That would be tough to explain.

"Wine, please."

I nodded at Yuki and waited on George to make up his mind. "I'll have wine, too."

"Got it."

I decided to join them. Electrolytes were good for replacing lost magic, but wine worked just a little bit better. Beer just made me pee.

By the time I got back to the living room the four of them had settled down on the couch and love seat and were quietly talking. I didn't want to butt in. I handed them their wine and went to check on Josie who was being awfully quiet in my bedroom.

She was reading on my bed again. "They're here."

"They staying?"

"In the house? Yes. Just until I hear from Mother."

"Let them know they can have my room. I'll bunk with you."

"That's very…accommodating of you. You feeling okay?"

"Har har."

I plopped down on the bed next to her, carefully sipping my wine. "How many do you think will come?"

"From home? Who knows."

"Are you excited?"

"Kind of, but mostly not. I like our little coven. It feels more real."

"Smaller has a tendency to do that," I answered.

"That's not it. It feels more like a family than a coven. We fight, we make up, we love. Okay, that's mostly you, but it's like watching your sister fight with her boyfriend."

"I'm glad I can be here for your entertainment."

My phone rang on the nightstand. I reached over and picked it up, answering. "Hello?"

"Dorothea?"

"This is she."

"I don't know if you remember me, but I'm Alista Dell…"

"Of course, I do. How are you?" I did remember her. She and her brother had sort of been the wallflowers of our coven. Both shy and timid.

"I am well. Alister and I heard from your mother you were looking for people to help out and possibly join your coven?"

I was kind of shocked. For them to pack up and move…was kind of out of the ordinary. The twins mostly kept to themselves. "I am. Are you interested?"

"Yes."

"Both of you?"

"Unfortunately," she said with a giggle.

If I remembered correctly, they owned one of the bakeries in Ashville. A cute homey one that specialized in desserts instead of breads… "You planning on moving the bakery here?"

"That is one of the main reasons we wish to relocate. There is an abundance of bakeries in town."

"I remember. So do my thighs."

"How is the market there?"

"Dismal, but I think you might be the perfect niche. And the real estate market never came back. You could buy or lease cheaply. How are your funds?"

"We've had an interested buyer for the property, not the business, for thirty years. We've been holding out. But this might be the perfect time to cave in. Would you be interested in having us?"

Hell yeah. And your cinnamon buns.

"That is most definitely a possibility. I'm making a list of those interested. So far, you're the first ones. Once I get an idea of who wants to come on a more permanent basis, and who wants to just help for a short time, we can schedule a meet and get the ball rolling. Does that sound good?"

"Most definitely. If you *are* looking for someone to help with the wards, I can come out there tomorrow and stay for a while. Alister can handle the shop for that long. And honesty, I need the break."

"Then fly into Syracuse. Text me your flight number and I'll pick you up. I'll take you up on *that* offer right now. You can even take a look around town at some properties. I know a good real estate agent…"

"That would be perfect. I'll text you shortly and hopefully see you tomorrow."

"Perfect. Thanks, Alista."

"No. Thank you!"

I stared at the phone for a second, not quite believing how well that worked out.

"Alista? Dell?"

I nodded. "She and her brother are interested in moving the bakery out here."

"Oh, my Lady! I can sell their pastries in the coffee shop, if their shop isn't too close to the bookstore. Wonder if they'd be interested in working something out."

"Talk to her tomorrow. She's flying out for a few weeks to help out the vampires."

"Really? She was always so *quiet.*"

"Who knows. Maybe this move will be good for them."

My phone rang again. And again. And several times after that. I spent the rest of the evening making a list of candidates. By the time I finally shut my ringer off and went to bed I had a list twelve people long.

Josie hadn't looked shocked at all.

CHAPTER 14

Wanting to be a rebel, I ordered something different, a hash brown and sausage omelet with no cheese. It was missing something, so I squirted a squiggle of ketchup on it. I let out a little *squee* at the first bite. I cut another forkful of omelet and slid it into my mouth, letting the tangy taste of ketchup fill me with happy.

The door opened and someone kissed my cheek. I looked up to see a smiling Jimmy, with his faithful cohort standing behind him.

"Morning, sexy," I said with a mouthful of omelet.

"Morning, beautiful. Mind if we share your booth?"

I scooted over. "I'd prefer it. Missed you," I said, swallowed, and kissed him on his lips.

"Morning, Dot."

"Morning, Dennis," I said and flashed him a grin. Hopefully without any eggs in my teeth.

"No kiss?"

I chuckled. "If you want one."

"Maybe later. I don't feel like leaning over the table. Probably make Jimmy all jealous and shit, anyway."

"Miss anything while we were working?"

"Only the fight of the century with Chief."

The both blinked in surprise. "All okay?"

I nodded. "Now. We made up."

Jimmy cocked a questioning eyebrow at me.

"Not that much."

He actually looked kind of disappointed. I rolled my eyes at him and took another bite of food. "Bought another house, our new friends from out of town joined my houseguests. Called my mother for some reinforcements, one is flying in today. I need to pick her up from the airport in an hour and a half. We also might be getting a bunch more coven members." I whispered the last part. "I've had quite a few requests to relocate from my old coven."

"Your mom okay with that?"

"She wouldn't have passed the word along if she weren't."

"Wow. More new people. Any as hot as you?" Dennis asked and leaned forward in his seat.

I blinked in surprise. "You think I'm hot?"

He rolled his eyes. "Everybody thinks you're hot. Quit being modest."

"You are just so sweet. You get two kisses now."

Marge stopped by the table. "You boys eating or just enjoying the scenery?"

"Burger and a chocolate malt." Jimmy ordered without looking at the menu.

"Patty melt and a chocolate shake."

"Have it out shortly."

"Kind of early for shakes. No?" I loved ice cream. Nay, I was addicted to it. I doubted I could ever have anything ice cream based before noon, though. Booze yes, ice cream no.

"Never too early," Jimmy said with a laugh and leaned over, planting a soft kiss on my neck that sent shivers all the way down.

"Knock it off. I don't want to have to drive to the airport all squishy."

"Want some company?" Jimmy asked with a hint of heat in his voice.

"Dennis? You want to go with me? We can leave this one here."

"Sure."

"Traitor!" Jimmy poked him with a fork from across the table.

"I'm kidding. You guys can come if you're bored."

Jimmy shot me a thoughtful look. It made me nervous. He was plotting something. Then he wiggled his eyebrows.

I rolled my eyes. "What are you, twelve?"

"You have no idea. He drives the other guys nuts at the station. Ask him about his dirty magazine collection, Dot. Go ahead."

"You like dirty magazines?"

"Maybe."

"He also likes to leave them everywhere. Mostly in the bathroom."

"Ew. TMI." The words came out of my mouth, but I liked the picture in my head.

"What? I get bored easily." He was horrible at defending himself.

"Read a book," I quipped.

"That's why I buy those magazines. They're just brimming with wonderful articles."

Ignoring him, I finished my omelet and chugged the rest of my coke. Grabbing my mug of coffee, I sat back while we waited for their food.

"So, what did you and Bill fight about," Jimmy asked concernedly.

"Jason was attacked by the rogue witches. He kind of had a shitfit that I was putting the coven in danger."

"He okay?" Dennis asked. I could hear the worry in his voice. I'm sure the thought of losing another one of our coven was a little more close to them, since they had lost their friend Richie.

"Yeah. He maintained the wards but got beat up doing it. That's why I'm picking up Alista. She's going to stay at the new house as a ward keeper. That way they'll last until help arrives."

"Alista?"

"She's from Ashville. She and her twin brother own a bakery. They're some of the ones thinking about moving here more permanently."

"She cute?"

I laughed at Dennis. "Yes, very. But quiet and shy."

He raised his eyebrows. "She have a boyfriend?"

"Not that I know of."

"Now I'm definitely going."

Their food came and they wolfed it down. Dennis chugged his milkshake. How, I don't know. I'd have been grabbing my head, screaming like a bitch, and running around in little circles. Two consecutive sips of *anything* frozen and I had instant brain freeze. It's the major reason I never got into frozen adult beverages. Keep the daiquiris, give me the rum.

Marge dropped off three separate checks. I grabbed them all and handed her my card.

"You need to stop doing that," Jimmy said, kind of put out.

"You guys are coming on a trip with me. I can buy your lunch."

"Blah blah blah. You always have an excuse to pay for everything."

"Fine. You can buy me dinner. Someplace romantic."

"Deal. Breakfast, too?" Jimmy grinned, brightly.

"Maybe."

"Lucky bastard." Dennis set his cup down and threw a wadded-up napkin at his head.

"Here you go, Hun. Don't know why you pay for these little ingrates."

"Thanks, Marge. Have a good one."

The boys slid out and Jimmy offered me his hand. He pulled me out of the cushioned seat and kissed me. "You taste good."

"Thanks." I smiled. He really was a sweetheart. "Come on, we need to get going."

"Want to take my truck?"

"No. I don't want her luggage to get snowed on." His truck did fit four or five people, but he didn't have a cover over the bed. And it smelled kind of funny. Like someone roasting fast food over a campfire. It wasn't pleasant, but I guess it was one of the hazards of being a fireman.

We headed for my SUV parked right outside the diner. I started it up and unlocked the doors right from the key fob. I should have started it when we were inside the diner and let the heat do its job. But the heated seats made up for it.

We got out of town and on to the highway. I flipped the radio on and started singing.

"You bought us lunch and now you're punishing us?"

"No. If I wanted to punish you, I would have reminded you that you could spend an evening alone and I could take Dennis out for dinner."

"I'm good with that," Dennis said from the back seat.

Jimmy leaned over, kissed me softly on the ear, and whispered, "It wouldn't be a punishment if you told me what happened after…"

His pervy nature was starting to rub off on me. My inner slut kind of liked that idea. It didn't even bother me that it was Dennis and not Chief…

Down, girl.

"Is it getting hot in here?"

"It is a little warm," Dennis said from the back seat again, not hearing our exchange.

Jimmy's hand settled on my thigh. He started nonchalantly sliding it up and down my leg. "I'm driving you know."

"All the fancy shit in this car and you're going to tell me you don't have cruise control?"

I sighed but set our speed for an even seventy-five.

He continued his gentle caresses on my leg. I shifted in my seat, enjoying his touch. When his fingers got a little too close to home plate, I scrunched my thighs together, trapping him from going any further. Or so I thought. He spread his fingers and his pinky slid home. I tried not to gasp as I shot him a dirty look. He just smiled innocently and started looking around at the scenery.

"Everything is so much prettier with the little bit of snow."

"It's supposed to warm up tomorrow and rain. That will make a nice mess of everything." Dennis didn't sound too happy about it.

"Should be fun driving. Remind me to stay home tomorrow. How warm?"

"Into the thirties, but then it's supposed to freeze again at night. Ten bucks say the guys on duty have to go out ten times for fender benders on Saturday."

"At least you guys are off."

They both nodded.

Jimmy got a little bolder with his pinky, letting a second finger help applying pressure to the front of my leggings. I let out a breath and he noticed, sporting a cocky little smile. He pulled my leg away from the other. I couldn't believe I let him do it.

His hand slid lower and closer, letting the tips of his fingers curl under me. His middle finger nestled into the crease in my pants and started caressing me. It would have been a little suspicious if Dennis could see his whole arm moving.

I turned my head and looked at him out of the corner of my eye, narrowing my lids.

I'll let you play, but I can't believe you're doing this.

He just broadened his smile and turned to look out the window again. "You look lovely, today. Can I ask you a question?" He turned back to look at my face as he increased the pressure with his finger.

"What?" I managed to get the word out without moaning.

"How come you don't wear skirts? You're always wearing leggings or jeans."

The little shit.

I could only imagine the trouble he would get me into if I wore a skirt. "It's winter. Cold."

Great, now I'm not even talking in complete sentences...

"Huh. I guess your legs would get cold. It would probably be hard to stay warm, huh?"

He forced the front of my leggings into me a little and rubbed his finger in the channel he'd created. I'd have bet hard cash I was going to end up with a spot on the front of them.

"Yes!" I answered his question and did *not* cry out in pleasure. I swear.

"You okay, Dot?" Dennis asked.

My face flushed and I nodded, meeting his eyes in the rear-view mirror.

"You don't sound okay. Your back hurting?" Jimmy chimed in next to me, being a little shit.

"Yeah. It's a little stiff," I managed to say and looked down at his lap. I wasn't wrong.

He was enjoying watching me squirm. Immensely. I focused on the road and tried to ignore the sensations spreading through me. I tried. It wasn't working. I could feel it starting. His fingers, and knowing Dennis was right behind me, were quickly becoming too much.

Jimmy turned to look at Dennis. "You happy to be off for a couple of days?"

"Hell yeah. You're not?" He sounded confused.

"Oh, I am. I especially love it when the next shift rolls in and we get to walk out of there. *Getting off* is my favorite feeling in the world."

No. He didn't.

I couldn't believe he even stressed the words. He was literally teasing me to a mind-blowing orgasm. What scared me more was the fact that I was letting him, with his best friend sitting behind me.

"Yeah. That's a good feeling," Dennis answered slowly, unsure what the hell was going on.

"You should thank Dennis for *coming* along with us, Dot."

That did it. I shuddered in my seat, managing not to scream, arch my back, and crash into the ditch alongside the highway. I breathed through my nose, letting it pass through me. I put my elbow on the door by the window and brought my fist to my lips.

"Thank you for coming, Dennis," I managed to squeak out after coming down.

"You're uh…welcome."

His voice was beside my ear. I gasped, not knowing when he had leaned forward. He was close enough to see *exactly* what was going on, too.

I backhanded Jimmy in the chest, and reaching down, grabbing his wrist. I moved it over to his lap. Too little, too late. I should have paid more attention to where Dennis was. "Jerk."

"Oh, shush. You know you liked it." He grinned at me from across the car.

"Sorry, Dennis."

"Don't worry about it, Dot. Not only is he a pervert, he loves embarrassing people. Especially his friends. That was kind of hot, by the way." He sounded okay, but his face was beat red, and his eyes shifted in every direction, avoiding eye contact…even in the mirror. I couldn't blame him. I'm sure my face was the same color as his.

Every time I ended up around Jimmy, I always think that there was no way I could ever be more embarrassed than I was right at that moment. He consistently proved me wrong. What's worse is I was really starting to like it. With Chief, it was understandable, but this was Dennis, his best friend. That scared me, too. And sent a shiver up my spine.

I pulled off at the rest area and parked without a word.

"Gotta pee?"

"Well I need to use the fucking bathroom, that's for certain."

I got out of the car and ran inside to clean myself up a little, leaving them in the running car. If Jimmy followed me in, we would definitely be late to the airport...

"Feel better?" He snickered as I got back in the car.

"Dryer, that's for sure."

His snicker turned into a full-blown chuckle.

Thankfully the rest of the drive to the airport was uneventful. I don't think I could handle anything more.

She was waiting curbside as we pulled in. Luckily, she hadn't changed at all since I saw her last month. Even though she was wearing a heavy winter coat, you could tell she was very thin, almost waif-like. Her blonde hair had been pulled up into its usual ponytail and hung out the back of her woolen hat. I waved as we parked in front of her and she flashed a cute little smile.

"Hi, Alista!" I shouted as I got out of the vehicle after popping the trunk.

"Greetings, Lady."

The poor girl was shaking. She wasn't used to harsh winters.

"Get in the car! Oh, my Lady, your lips are blue. Were you waiting long?"

"Plane was early. Of course."

"Why didn't you wait inside?"

"I didn't want you to miss me."

I gave her a quick hug and opened the door behind Jimmy, practically shoving her inside. "Turn the heat up for her!"

I grabbed her suitcase, set it in the trunk, and got back in the driver's seat. "Alista, meet Jimmy and Dennis." I pointed to them as I said their names. "Guys, this is Alista Dell."

"Welcome to town." Jimmy nodded from the front seat.

Dennis offered her his hand. "Pleasure to meet you."

I smiled and pulled away from the curb, heading home.

The vampires wandered around the house, each claiming a room. They'd hit it off with Alista almost immediately. I was happy and kind of shocked because of her shy nature.

I spoke to Yuki and George about furnishings, offering to take them furniture shopping, but they insisted that Mr. Abernathy had set up a bank account for them to cover living improvements, as well as to cover their day to day expenses. I nodded, they didn't look like they would accept any more help.

"The house was more than enough. Mr. Abernathy thanks you," George said curtly. "We have a truck full of our stuff coming from home tonight. We can order for Amir and Yvette and have it delivered. We already spoke to Alista about accepting the delivery."

While they were looking around, I took Alista outside and familiarized her with the wards and their feeding points. She picked it up quickly and even sent a bit of power into them, just to watch them flare.

With that, my work with them was over. Unless they were attacked. Though I still needed to uphold my part of the bargain with Mr. Abernathy. I'd take care of that tomorrow.

"You all set?" I checked with Alista, one last time.

"Yep. They each picked a room, but I'm going to stay in Yuki's room until this is over. She doesn't mind bunking with George."

"I bet she doesn't. He's cute."

"And gay, and her cousin. That's why she doesn't mind sharing a room with him."

"Oh. I thought they were a couple."

"No. I asked. I thought the same thing."

"Well, I need to get going. You sure you don't need anything?"

"No. I have money, I'll order takeout or something."

"Okay. You have my number if there's any problems or change your mind. I'm serious. If you need *anything*, let me know."

"Dennis said the same thing."

I smiled. While I was happy a little bit of romance might be flaring for the two of them, I had to slay the green monster welling up inside me. It took me a moment to get over that. Quickly, I blurted, "He's cute and a sweetheart."

"He is."

"Ten bucks says he stops by tonight to check on you." I put air-quotes around the word check.

"Nope. Not taking that bet."

I chuckled and headed for my car. Mildly convinced one problem had been dealt with.

CHAPTER 15

The house seemed so empty. Candace was at work, the vampires had moved out, and Josie went to the bar. I saw her hastily scribbled note telling me to meet her if I wanted. How she got there, I didn't have a clue. If Jimmy wasn't on his way to pick me up, I might have met her.

I jumped in the shower quick and had just wrapped a towel around myself when the doorbell rang. I padded out of my room and almost slipped on the hardwood floor, catching the couch and saving myself from a nasty bruise. I finally made it to the door without injuring myself.

"You have horrible timing."

"What? Why?" Jimmy laughed.

"I almost killed myself getting to the door. You couldn't have rung the doorbell a minute later?"

"My bad," he said as he entered, shutting the door behind him.

"Where are we going?"

"It's a surprise."

I narrowed my eyes at him. "I don't like surprises."

"You did today…"

I rolled my eyes and scoffed. "I'm going to get dressed."

"Can I ask you something first?" He sounded serious. I was almost worried.

"What?"

He grabbed the hand not holding the front of the towel and pulled me over to the couch, sitting me down gently and kneeling in front of me.

"If the words will, you, and marry me come out of your mouth, so help me goddess, I will punch you."

He tilted his head and then realized the position we were in and snorted. "No! Goddess, no. Sorry, I just wanted to talk to you for a second."

"Okay. Good."

"I hope."

"You hope what?"

"That the conversation we're about to have is good."

"I won't know unless you actually start."

"Was today good for you?"

Not where I thought he was going to go with it. "You're worried I'm mad because you made me come in front of Dennis?"

"Yes."

"Little late to worry about it now, but no. I'm not mad. Embarrassed to all hell, but not mad. As long as you understand, I don't mind your games as long as it's somebody I'm comfortable with. Chief, fine. Dennis, pushing it. Okay?"

He breathed a sigh of relief. "Okay, good. I'm sorry, I just get caught up in the moment of things sometimes, and Dennis kind of yelled at me after. I was getting *the vibe* that you were enjoying it, but it made me wonder."

I spread my legs exposing myself in front of him. His eyes immediately drank in the sight. "I'm going to be very honest with you, and don't let this go to that thick little head of yours." I paused to gently rub the front of his slacks with the tips of my toes. "You let me in on another little secret I didn't know about myself today. I liked being watched. I liked you showing me off. The other night at dinner with Chief was *hot*, but this was… Yeah. Especially having to hold it in like that. Made it ten times better."

162

He smiled and leaned forward, kissing me on my lips. "And that just made it a hundred times hotter, knowing how much more you liked it than I thought. You just made me very happy."

He lowered himself a little and kissed my neck, tugging my towel apart and going even lower. He gently kissed my right nipple and the center of my chest, before reaching the left and flicking his tongue across it. He kissed my tummy and belly button, but before he got any lower, I stopped him.

"I want to get to dinner before they close."

"One more second…"

He continued his journey south and kissed me once more, right at the point where my patch of pubic hair met the top of my lips. I shivered at the intimacy of it.

He stood up and offered me his hands, but I shook my head. Instead, I unzipped him, reached in, and pulled him out the front of his pants. He was semi-hard from seeing me naked and planting little kisses over my body, but he was hot in my hand. I leaned forward and kissed the tip before putting him back in his pants. It had gotten a lot harder to accomplish. There wasn't anything semi about his state after that.

"That was fucking hot."

"Figured you'd like that. Tit for tat."

"I like that expression. When I was younger, I thought it meant show me your boobs and I'll buy you a tattoo. This is much better. I like your tits, but I don't know if I'd like you with tats."

"You're impossible," I said with a short laugh. "I'm going to go get dressed. You wait *here*."

"Yes'm."

I grabbed my towel as I stood up. I hadn't washed my hair, as this was my second shower of the day, so it would only take me a few minutes to get ready.

Panties, leggings, and a soft sweater later, I walked out of the bedroom. He took one look at me and shook his head.

"What?"

"This is a *date*. You have to dress the part. Come with me." He got up, walked over to me, grabbed my hand and pulled me back into the bedroom.

I stood in front of my dresser, staring at myself in the mirror as he stood behind me, fingers on his chin. He looked like a sculptor staring at a hunk of marble and visualizing the lines of his strikes.

Reaching down, he grabbed the hem of my sweater, lifting it up over my head and arms. He totally messed up the pony-tail it had taken me agonizing seconds to put in.

He shook his head at the bra, too. With a quick snap of his fingers, it was unhooked, and he was letting it fall forward and off my arms.

"Somebody's had a lot of practice," I grumbled, jealousy flaring through me.

"Shush. Later."

He bent down and lifted one foot and then the other, sliding my boots off. Finally, he rolled his eyes and pulled down my leggings, holding them as I stepped out of them. Standing up he looked at me over my shoulder in the mirror.

"Beautiful," he whispered.

"Thank you, but I'm not going to dinner wearing panties."

"Okay."

He pushed them down over my ass and onto the floor.

"That's not what I meant."

"Shush. Now I must dress you."

He walked into my closet, flicking on the light. I heard the hangers sliding as he said, "No, no, no, goddess no, hell no, no. Aha!"

I almost didn't want to look when he walked out carrying my little red dress that I hadn't worn in almost two years. I loved it, but it was a tad bit revealing. I'd bought it for a Yule party and never worn it again.

"That's *very* skimpy, Jimmy."

"I know. Arms up!"

I sighed, tried not to laugh, and put my hands in the air.

He got it over my hands and slowly worked it down my body, taking his time and caressing me *everywhere.* When it was over my hips, he turned me around and ran his hands over it, smoothing it out.

"Perfection."

"You want to pick the thong I'm going to wear?"

He leaned in until his nose was millimeters from mine, his eyes boring into mine. "No. You do not get to wear panties this evening."

"I'm not wearing *this* dress out to diner without panties, Jimmy."

His stare turned into a smile. "Yes. Yes you are…"

"Why should I?"

"Because I told Chief you wouldn't be wearing any…"

I shifted as wetness began to collect at my opening. It wasn't enough to be uncomfortable, but it was enough to give me a chill.

What is he doing to me and why do I like it so fucking much?

"You insist?"

"I do."

"Fine. Let's go."

"I thought that would change your mind…"

∞ ∞ ∞

"Lambresco's?"

"A fine Italian eatery serving the greater Cedar Fall's area since 1953…"

"Been here a couple of times?"

"Maybe. I like sketti."

I laughed. He really was too cute. I gave him a kiss for the effort. He held the door and I swished past him, my dress flaring where it stuck out of my heavy jacket. Jimmy took it off me as soon as the door closed behind him. Taking his off, he hung both on the brass hooks by the door.

The place smelled delightful and I wasn't even a huge fan of Italian food, or pasta, in general. An older Italian woman lazily sauntered up from the back.

"Hello, Jimmy."

"Hi, Maria. Table for two, please."

She grabbed two laminated menus and lead us to a table in the back. At least there weren't many people in the place if things got…interesting.

"Drinks?"

"Vino for the lady, and I'll have a beer, please."

Jimmy slid into the booth motioning for me to sit beside him, the plastic covering frigid against the back of my legs.

"You suck," I said after Maria left.

"Why?"

"The seat is *cold*."

He chuckled as I picked up the menu and started glancing through it, trying to find something that didn't come with, or was made entirely out of, pasta.

"Chicken picatta. That sounds nummy. Even comes with grilled zucchini."

"That's a good thing?"

"Not a huge fan of pasta."

"And I picked Italian. I'm sorry, Dot. I didn't know."

"It's fine! Don't worry." I even leaned in, giving him a long sensuous kiss. "Learning new things about each other makes me happy."

Maria brought our drinks and I took a tentative sip of the wine. It wasn't bad. "What kind of vino?" I asked Jimmy after Maria left.

"Chianti."

"I thought you drank that with fava beans and liver?"

"Um, what?" Jimmy stared at me like I'd grown an extra head.

"Never mind." I set my menu down, feeling a little silly.

A few moments later and the front door opened. I could hear the chime, but couldn't see who walked in. I got my answer when Maria walked Chief back to the booth *exactly* diagonal from ours. She even set his menu down on the side of the booth facing us. I wouldn't have been surprised if she tackled him and set him on that side if he tried to move. I cocked an eyebrow at Jimmy.

"Isn't that weird. Of all the open booths she set him right by us. Wonder why?" I asked dryly.

He didn't even try to look innocent.

Chief didn't speak, just nodded hello.

I tilted my head to him and picked up my menu again, just for shits and giggles. It might have been because I had no idea what I was supposed to be doing. I could pretend to be a normal person eating in a restaurant. Yep.

Jimmy touched my leg. "Nervous?"

"Yes."

"Good. It will make it better."

"It will make what better? What am I going to do? Flash him again?"

"You'll see."

I made sure my legs were closed tightly. Maria came to get Chief's drink order. I was kind of shocked when he ordered wine instead of his normal beer.

She wrote it down and walked over to us. "Ready to order?"

"Sure thing," Jimmy replied, picking up his menu. "I'll do the spaghetti, garden sauce, and let's do the meatballs."

"Soup or salad?"

"Soup. Italian wedding."

"And for you?"

"Chicken picatta, salad."

She nodded and picked up the menus.

Jimmy leaned over and nibbled my ear. I almost screamed, and not in a good way. I was on edge and he knew it.

Chuckling, he kissed it gently. "Calamari."

"You want squid?"

"No. There is no chance in hell I would ever eat it, so there is zero chance you will hear me say that word again tonight."

"Okay."

"That word is for you."

"I hate that shit, too. It's like chewing a fishy tire."

"Good. Then you won't *accidentally* say it."

"Oh. It's my safe word, huh?"

He nodded. "You say it and the game stops."

My heart fluttered a little. Things were about to get dangerous enough I might need a safe word. It fluttered more because he wanted me to feel safe, even as I was walking the sword's edge. I gave him a wicked smile and nodded.

I rubbed my face against his shoulder before reaching over and taking a sip of wine. Jimmy reached down and began rubbing my leg again. I leaned back a little and enjoyed the feeling.

"So how much did it cost you to have Maria seat Chief in the best seat in the house?"

"Told her I'd double her tip."

"You called ahead?"

"Yep."

Suspicion clouded my brain. "You do this often?"

"Not in a very long time and those did not go well."

"Hard to find someone as pervy as you, huh?"

"Took me thirty-five years…"

That earned him an, "Awww." Then I realized he had just called me a pervert. A sense of indignancy started to settle in my chest but evaporated quickly.

I guess I can live with that.

168

I gasped as his hand slid up under my dress, he almost made it to the homeland when he pulled his hand out of my lap, taking a sip of beer. His movement had left my dress up around my waist. If my thighs hadn't been together, Chief could have seen everything. He must have gotten a good enough view to tell I wasn't wearing panties. He nearly spilled his wine.

I reached down to pull it back down when Jimmy grabbed my hand, entwining his fingers in mine. "Did I mention how beautiful you look in that dress?"

He didn't want me covering up.

Fine.

"Yes, but feel free to tell me again."

"You look amazing. When I saw you standing in front of the mirror, saw the silk clinging to your every curve, showing every detail of that glorious body underneath it…I almost took you right there. I almost couldn't contain myself. We'll have to try that. The dresser looks like it would be *exactly* the right height."

"Yeah, but my legs would be in the way."

"Not if they were over my shoulders…"

I gasped, the image alone sending gooseflesh down my arms.

"See. Just as pervy as me."

"Wanting to get fucked on a dresser hardly qualifies."

"Fine. We'll see just how much of a perv you are by the end of dinner."

I used Maria dropping off our soup and salad as an excuse to flip down my dress. I didn't mind showing off for Chief. Doing it for a fifty-something Italian waitress just didn't do it for me.

Jimmy spooned some of the soup in his mouth. "Wow. This is amazing, want to try?"

"No, thank you."

I took a bite of the salad and made *mmm* noises. The dressing was *really* good. "Okay. I'm impressed. I could come here and drink the creamy dressing and be happy."

Jimmy spit the spoonful of soup he'd just put in his mouth.

"Oops." I hadn't thought about what I was saying.

It took all of thirty-seconds for the game to begin again. As soon as Maria left Chief's table with his order, Jimmy's hand neglected his spoon and found my leg again. I thought he was going to sit there idly and play, but he grabbed his spoon in his left hand and resumed eating. I stared at him in shock and then for a different reason when his finger slipped between my thighs. He began lightly running it through my tuft of red hair.

I focused on my salad and getting the pieces to my mouth without hitting myself with the fork. Then he parted my legs. Not just a little either, he pulled my left leg over to his, my right leg mimicking its angle on its own. Chief gave up pretending not to stare, his eyes focusing on my juncture with open want and need as Jimmy just kept sliding his hand up and down my thigh.

I saw Maria bringing the chief his salad and closed my legs. As soon as she walked away, I opened them again on my own.

"Good girl," Jimmy whispered in my ear.

I continued to eat like that, glancing up occasionally to stare into Chief's eyes. When he saw me looking at him, he would look up at my eyes and back down, wetting his lips. I could almost feel his tongue on my flesh.

Jimmy leaned in, his warm breath tickling my ear. "See how hot he's getting? That was my intention the other night. Look at his pant leg."

I did. Sure enough, I could see him straining against the material, rigid and long.

I'd been so focused on my hunger I almost didn't notice Maria walking our way with two plates of food. I barely got my legs together when she got close enough to see. She may have blinked once or twice but gave no other indication she had seen anything.

"Spaghet for the gentleman, and the picatta for the lady. Can I get you some more wine or beer?"

I shook my head. My drink, forgotten, was still over half-full.

"I'm good, too. Thanks, Maria."

She smiled and walked away. I opened the theater for Chief once again, lifting the red curtain a little higher as well. Grabbing my knife and fork, I cut a small piece of chicken off and popped it in my mouth. The lemon caper sauce was perfect. I'd never had it before, but would certainly come back again for it.

Jimmy twirled his spaghetti with his left hand, and put the ball in his mouth, returning his hand to my lap. I expected him to tone it down while we ate. He didn't. He slid his hand down over me, letting three fingers caress me. One down the middle and two on either side of my lips. He pressed them together as he began to move his hand around. My wetness had made me incredibly slippery and he was using it to his advantage.

My hand shook as I tried to feed myself. I looked up at Chief pitifully, the sensations in my pussy drowning out everything around me. He'd given up just watching and was lightly rubbing the length of himself through his pants.

"He's rubbing his cock for you," Jimmy murmured, his voice hot and sultry. "He can't help it. You've turned him on that much."

I turned my gaze to Jimmy with assuredly glassy eyes. I could barely see.

"No, Dot. Don't look at me. This is our date, but this show is for him. Watch him. Show him how much pleasure you're in."

I did, but not before my lips met his in a sloppy kiss.

Then I did look at Chief as my breath came in ragged gasps. I almost cried out when his middle finger slipped inside. I managed to stop myself, but not before a series of low pitched *uh* sounds filtered through.

Jimmy slowed his pace, lightly running his fingers through my wetness. I could barely breathe. "You should eat. Your food is going to get cold."

I shook my head, trying to ignore the sensuous feelings from his grazing fingertips. I cut off a piece of parmesan crusted zucchini and brought it to my lips. As soon as it was in my mouth, his finger rubbed my clit. My jaw clenched, crunching the mouthful of food. And so, it continued until most of my dinner was finished. Then I noticed Chief's food in front of him and him chewing. Maria had brought it and I hadn't even noticed.

The thought flushed my face with heat. I wanted to bury my face in my hands as it caused me to get even wetter.

"Yes, she saw you."

"I can't believe I didn't even see her."

"Want to know what she did?"

"No. Please don't tell me."

"She smiled."

"She did?"

"Yes."

At least I didn't have to worry about her calling the police. Especially since he was in the booth next to us watching the show.

I'd finished my dinner. Maria was walking toward us and this time I did close my legs and look everywhere but her direction. She put another glass of wine down in front of me and a plate of strawberries. Jimmy had obviously been up to no good again.

She walked away without a word. "What are the strawberries for, Jimmy?"

"Dessert."

I had a bad feeling, but I spread my legs again, anyway. That wasn't good enough for Old Jimbo, though. He reached under my leg and lifted it up over his as he scooted a bit closer to me. Chief had an unobstructed view of everything.

"Maria won't be back until I signal her for the check. This is dessert and alone time. Just the two of you."

I reached over and grabbed my half-glass of wine and chugged it in one gulp. The second followed the first right after.

Jimmy grabbed a strawberry off the plate. I expected him to feed it to me, but I should have known better than that. Instead, he teased me with it, letting it slide across my lips. The moment I tried to take a bite, he pulled it back out of reach.

He let it glide gently over my chin and rested it against my bottom lip. "Bite."

Half expecting him to pull it away, I did, gasping at the sweetness of the flesh. He fed me with one hand and reached down with the other, rough fingers gliding gently across me. Dessert became a sweet, sensual game until there was only one strawberry left.

"*Jimmy*," I made his name a plea.

He grabbed the strawberry and slid it under the table. It slid over me, went inside me, and gently swirled before being plucked and set on the now empty plate in front of me.

"I bet Chief would love a taste. Go give it to him."

I didn't know if I could stand, let alone walk, but I tried. I gripped the table with one hand and the plate in the other, almost falling across the empty aisle to his table. "Dessert," I managed to say simply before going back to my seat.

I sat back down, and my face fell into my hands. I was crazy with lust, want, and need.

"Lay back against me."

I turned and did just that, resting my head on his shoulder and watching Chief eat his dessert and rub himself some more. He had to be close to coming. I could see it on his face.

"Put one leg up on the booth and the other on the floor, please."

I did just that, hoping he had an ounce of pity in his heart for what I was going through. I didn't care how exposed I was or who could walk by. I wanted my happy ending.

Chief stopped chewing when Jimmy reached down and pulled my dress up to my belly button before sliding his hand down over my mound and parting my flesh with his fingers. He rubbed me, hooking his middle finger and letting it plunge into me as he caressed all of me.

I didn't last long, and Jimmy knew my state well enough to cover my mouth with his hand as he brought me to oblivion. It began as a low panting and then a moan before becoming a wordless scream muffled by his palm as my reality shattered.

He rubbed my clit through the orgasm as I whimpered into his hand as my hips bucked and thrashed. I panted myself back to reality, tapping his hand to let him know I was okay.

Chief got up from the table, calmly walked past us to the bathroom.

"Go."

I sat up and blinked giving him a questioning glare.

"Don't make him do it himself. I want you to swallow every drop, too."

I nodded and gave him a little smile.

I headed, for the first time in my life, into the men's room. He was there waiting for me, ass against the sink and cock out. I walked, how I was walking I have no idea, over to him, hiking the front of my dress up. I grabbed him and rubbed the tip over me, hearing his jagged breaths as pleasure flowed through me in waves. It was only a few seconds before his eyes pleaded with me. I dropped to the ground in front of him, taking him into my mouth as he exploded. I swallowed and swallowed and then swallowed more, not minding the taste in the least. Almost wanting it.

When he was finished, I stood up, tucked him back into his pants, turned around, and walked back to my table without a word.

CHAPTER 16

I woke up the next morning, panting and reliving dinner in my dream.

Reality had seen me go back to the table and sitting there demurely as he paid the bill and we walked out of the restaurant hand in hand. He even kissed me as we got into his truck. Another shock from the man that was Jimmy. He didn't even bat an eyelash. Then he took me home, practically carried me to my bed, and made slow sensuous love to me. It had been tender and almost as amazing as the restaurant. He tucked me in and kissed me goodnight, naked under the covers before heading home, complaining about a furniture delivery in the morning.

The dream saw Chief following us home, a glowing invitation clutched firmly in his hand. The both of them had followed me inside and did things to me I never would have considered just a month ago and I loved every sweaty, salty moment of it. I almost ached as I sat up in bed, not alone.

Even though the house was empty again, Josie and Candace were in their usual spots on either side of me. Candace smiling knowingly at me as she clung to my waist.

"Have a good night?"

"Maybe. Why?"

"You smell different and you were moaning almost all night long."

"Shhh. I don't wanna talk about it." I smiled and ran my fingers through her hair.

She nodded and lay her head back down on her pillow.

I slid out under the comforter at the end of the bed, leaving them were they were, Candace never ceasing to amaze me. I shook my head at her prone form and went into my bathroom to take a shower.

I let the hot water wash away the night's festivities. It was going to be a *long* time before anything like that ever happened again. I hoped Jimmy enjoyed it. I hoped Chief enjoyed it. I was getting away from the different flavors and sticking to vanilla for a while. The embarrassment during the act was like a potent drug. The embarrassment *after* felt like withdrawals. Standing under the spray, I rubbed my face for a good five minutes before feeling well enough to face the coffee maker. The world was going to have to wait a bit longer.

Unable to find my robe, I wrapped a towel around me and another around my hair in a twist before heading straight for coffee.

"That's it. I'm buying a Keurig." I had never wanted to shatter something more in my life. Every time I made coffee, I got angrier. After coffee…Amazon. I could wait two days for the solution to my crisis. It's not like Cedar Falls had a Wally World.

The soft knock on my door stopped my heart. I really didn't want to answer it. Not even a little bit. I thought I could ignore it until someone knocked again, a little louder.

"Fuck."

I padded barefoot to the door and peeked at who was on the other side. Of course, it was Chief. The man had no sense of decorum.

Doesn't he know there is a minimum three-day waiting period between awkward sexual displays and personal interaction?

"Yes?" I called through the door.

"Dot?"

"Yeah."

"Um…can I come in?"

"Do you have to?"

"Do you not want me to?"

I sighed. "Fine."

I unlocked the door and walked back to the coffee maker. Standing there in silence, mesmerized by the slow drip, I watched him come around the other side and stand behind the counter.

"Are you okay?"

"I don't know yet. I'll let you know in a day or two when I can think straight."

He wisely chose not to chuckle, laugh, or smirk. I knew because I was watching closely for any signs. He set his phone and other things down on the counter and walked around it, wrapping me in his arms.

He also chose wisely by not telling me it would be okay or any other platitudes. He just held me and rocked me while we both watched the coffee maker.

"Are you embarrassed, sad, angry, or regretful."

"Can I be all four?"

"No. You shouldn't be any of them."

"Chief, last night…"

"Was a *lot* of fun. You were having the time of your life or you would have stomped off. Right?"

"Huh?"

"If Jimmy had asked you to do one single *thing* you didn't want to do, it wouldn't have happened, right?"

"Right?"

"So why are you feeling bad about it now. It was just us. Maybe a little of the waitress, but Jimmy has known her since he was a little kid. She's not going to say anything to anyone. It's not like we did it in the diner. So, let it go. I know I had fun."

I pulled back a little. "Did you?"

"Couldn't you tell?"

"You didn't think it was awkward?"

"Fuck no. I almost wanted to sit on the other side of you and play, too."

"Maybe next time," I joked and pulled away, dumping a cup of coffee in my mug. I set the pot down for Chief and went and sat on the couch, sipping slowly.

"Maybe," he called out as he was filling a mug.

He came and sat down across from me. "I figured you'd be doing this. Even Jimmy did. He texted me from his furniture delivery to go check on you when I was halfway here."

"He did?"

"Yes."

"You both care for me a lot, don't you?"

"More than you can imagine. I'd place a bet on it."

"You'd have to be able to prove it, and I don't see that happening anytime soon."

"Hundred bucks says I can."

Intrigued, I nodded, figuring easy money. It's not like I couldn't afford the loss and even if he could prove it, I still won. I doubted it, but I could use it right now.

"Your phone in your room?"

I nodded. "Nightstand."

Chief paused at the doorway, noticing the sleeping Josie and Candace in my bed. He tiptoed silently in and came back out a minute later with a questioning look on his face.

"They sleep with me sometimes."

"You sleep between your best friend and her girlfriend?"

"Yes. Platonically. They're snuggle-whores."

He chuckled and handed me my phone. "Text him."

"Jimmy?"

"Duh."

I unlocked my phone and brought up his chain of messages. "What should I say?"

"Type, Jimmy. I want to know exactly how you feel about me, right now."

180

My fingers started typing but slowed the further I got into the sentence, fear gripping my chest like a vice. I handed Chief the phone. "You do it."

"Scared?"

"Terrified."

He did it and hit send, handing the phone back to me. It took all of eight seconds to read his reply.

I love you. Is that okay?

I felt the tear roll down my cheek.

"Get your answer?"

"Half of it."

I think I love you, too. Thank you. Don't bring this up again and don't say it again unless I ask. Or I'll bust your nuts, I typed jokingly. Not ready to deal with the L word.

Deal

I smiled and set my phone down on the table.

"Half your question?"

"How do you feel about me right at this moment?"

"Shit, Dot. If you had asked me a week ago…" He chuckled softly.

"Chief, tread lightly."

"I would have told you that I doubted I had the capacity to love another woman again as long as I lived."

"And now?"

"I would have called myself a liar."

I blushed as I took another sip of my coffee. "Guess I owe you a hundred."

"Do you want me to say it to you?"

I shook my head. "No. I'm happy with that."

"And…"

"I think you're a pain in the ass."

I should have grabbed my phone to take a picture of his face at that moment. It was totally worth it to see the look of utter shock on his face.

"But I feel the same," I added with a smile.

He started breathing again, almost hyperventilating. He even clutched his heart dramatically.

181

"Does it bother you that it's not just you?"

"Again, a week ago it might have, but I like to think I've grown…matured." He held out his hand and looked up at the ceiling like a classically trained actor.

He made me chuckle.

He always made me chuckle. And swear. And scream. In good ways and bad. I couldn't imagine living life without either of them at that point in time.

My boyfriends.

There. I said it.

"Thanks, Bill."

"You're welcome. Now can we talk about how absolutely amazingly hot you were last night?"

"No."

∞ ∞ ∞

Candace grabbed a shopping cart and pushed it between us as we walked through the entrance to Wally World. We'd driven thirty minutes to Amersville. Everybody made fun of the place in Cedar Falls, but at least they had a Super Center.

I'd given up on my Amazon plan. I wanted instant gratification and decided to shop for the new damn coffee maker, live and in person. That and I needed a few hundred other things and fixings for Thanksgiving.

Candace was off for the weekend and judging by the amount of people wandering the store, so was everybody else.

"I'm going to go look at candy," Josie said excitedly.

"She's right here," I said and pointed between us.

"You're a real comodian."

"You talkin' shit?"

We'd been using the same joke since the 90s. It never got old. I smiled at her and then offered to take the cart from Candace. She shook her head and walked along with me. Josie didn't mind and practically skipped away.

"You know, one of these days you're going to hurt her feelings if you keep clinging to me instead of her," I whispered to her.

"She knows."

"What?"

"That I love her. I told her. But, you are our Lady."

"And that means?"

"We are yours. Both of us."

I ran my fingers through her hair. She was as fae as they came and a little strange, but sweet as sugar. I just wish I knew more about her.

Maybe this is a good time to find out.

Self, sometimes you're so smart you scare me.

"How old are you, Candace?"

"I'll be nearly seven hundred in a month-and-a-half."

I stopped walking. My feet refused to carry me another step.

"Say that again?"

She looked up at me and blinked. "I'm nearly seven-hundred-years-old?"

It was my turn to blink rapidly.

"Did you think I was younger?"

I nodded. Slowly.

She gave a light giggle. "Please keep it between you and me. I don't like to spread that around."

I nodded. Slowly.

Shaking my head, my feet finally obeyed. "Head toward the appliances. We're getting the coffee maker first, so I don't forget."

"Aye."

"Where were you born?"

"Denmark."

"Ahh, so that was Danish."

"My canting?"

I nodded.

"Yes."

She left it at that.

"When did you come to America?"

Her face darkened. "1793."

"I won't pry. I'm sorry."

"No. I don't mind if you ask, I just fear the memories when I remember."

"You haven't had an easy life. Even a fool can tell that much."

"I was a slave for much of it."

Good job, Dot.

I stopped and touched her shoulder, wrapping her in a hug in the middle of the store. "Damn it, Candace. I'm sorry. I won't ask anything more, but if you ever want to talk about it, I'd love to listen to your story."

She nodded against my chest. "It is okay, Lady. It was long ago, and I like my life now. Especially now."

I kissed her forehead, ignoring the looks from the strangers around us.

We finally found the coffee makers. The biggest, baddest model found its way into our cart. Along with two giant boxes of coffee pods, an espresso maker, water filters, espresso beans, a grinder, two bottles of flavored syrup, and a milk frothing pitcher. When she wasn't looking, I tossed in two boxes of mint hot chocolate Candace had been eyeballing but was too afraid to ask for. She noticed them, and the cutest smile crossed her face. I winked at her.

"Guess we're going to need another cart. I should have grabbed two. Let's check on Josie and make sure she doesn't have a cartful of candy, and we can grab one before we finish shopping."

Candace nodded.

It took nearly ten minutes to find her, and she had a cart, but it wasn't full, *yet.* I staged an intervention. I snuck up behind her and grabbed the cart when she was bent down grabbing a bag of Twizzlers. "That's enough, sugar fiend."

"But, Mommm."

Candace giggled.

I transferred half the candy to the other cart and put the rest on a shelf. The stuff I hated. "This is why we have to keep an eye on her at all times. Okay, Candace?"

"Yes, Lady."

"Big meanie. The both of you."

"You want diabeetus? Cuz this is how you get diabeetus, Josie."

"We can't get diabetes, and you know it."

"Better safe than sorry. Let's hit the toiletries and then food."

"I need some more candles, too."

"What did I tell you about open flames, Josie."

"Not to roast marshmallows in the house and I haven't."

"Okay. One candle. But make it pumpkin."

"Two and you get the pumpkin, I want apple pie."

"Deal."

We shook on it. I smiled as I stocked up on shampoo and conditioner, deodorant, razors, moisturizing cream, and other various necessities I would have given an arm and a leg for eighty years ago. Back then we had soap. And we liked it.

Without realizing it, I'd been craving normalcy with every part of me. This was as normal as normal got. At least without medication. I was probably the first person in history to find a trip to Walmart relaxing.

We picked up the stuff we were running short of in the house. Cedar Falls had a local grocery store that we'd been shopping at since day one. Now we were buying in bulk. The second cart was filled almost as quickly as the first and we needed a third just for the food for Thanksgiving.

Laughing, the three of us pushed our carts to the checkout line. The cashier gave me the total and I winced, pulling out my bankcard. Before I could slip it in the card reader, Candace inserted hers.

"Candace, no!"

185

"*Ik spreek geen Engels.*"

"Did you just tell me you don't speak English?" The words were foreign, but I could pick a couple out.

She nodded and grinned at me as she punched in her PIN. The cashier smiled and handed her the receipt. I wanted to swat her.

"Why would you do that?" I pouted at her.

"Because. You do so many nice things for me, it was a chance to do something nice. Do not worry. I do not squander my money, like some." She shot Josie a narrow-eyed glance.

"Hey. Candy is a sound investment toward my happiness."

"Yes. I am."

I lost it. I started laughing in the middle of the store. I saw one woman jump in the self-checkout line next to us and I'm sure there were others. I didn't care.

"Come on. Let's get all this stuff in the car if we can."

CHAPTER 17

Josie and Candace were cuddled on the couch and Jimmy was sitting on the loveseat next to me as the movie droned on. I hadn't been paying any attention after losing interest in the first ten minutes. I knew how the story ended before we started. Cocky asshole ship designers versus an iceberg. What did they think was going to happen? And the love story kind of made me want to puke.

I was on my sixth game of sudoku.

I wasn't very good at it, but it had a certain entertainment value.

Wanna go make out?

Jimmy's text caught me off guard and I snorted.

I swear you are twelve. Make out? Really?

We wouldn't be the only ones…

What do you mean? For a moment, I thought he wanted to invite the girls or Chief along.

Josie and Candace. Look at the blanket and Candace's face.

I brought my phone up a little and looked at them over the top of it. They were spooning on the couch and had a blanket over them. Josie's one arm was sticking out holding the TV remote, but her other was under the blanket. Her elbow was moving up and down in a rhythmic motion. Candace wasn't staring at the TV and you could see the tiniest movement of her hips while she breathed rapidly through her mouth. It didn't take a rocket scientist to figure out what was going on.

Not like I can say anything about it. I'd be the biggest hypocrite on earth, I sent back.

Either way, it's kind of hot.

Candace buried her face in her arm and shuddered.

Damn. I wanted to see her O face, he texted again.

I rolled my eyes. He was such a…man. By all rights, I should have been angry for watching, but it seemed like everybody in my life had a voyeur or exhibitionist streak to them, including me. I just let it go.

Candace lifted her head and caught my gaze. She didn't blush like I would have expected, instead she gave me a grin. Apparently, she fit into *both* categories. I gave her a tiny smile and went back to my sudoku.

Now I'm hard.

I snorted at Jimmy's text and then his phone started ringing. Mine did, too. It was Alista.

"They're here, attacking the wards."

"On my way." I shut off the phone and jumped up, grabbing keys, jacket, and boots.

The other three were right behind me, all piling into my SUV. Jimmy was still on the phone with Dennis, who just happened to be visiting Alista. "He says they're not getting through the wards, especially not with the two of them feeding them."

"Tell him I owe him dinner for helping. How's Alista holding up."

"How you guys holding up? Dot says she owes you dinner."

I hit the main road and gunned it, heading away from town. "Josie, call Chief."

"I texted him already. He's on his way."

"Hang on guys, just a little bit longer," I whispered.

"Dennis says they're fine but getting a little tired."

"Tell him we're halfway there."

"Did you hear her?"

Blue lights started flashing behind me as a cop car turned in behind us. I fervently hoped it was Chief or I was going to have some serious explaining to do once I stopped. I kept glancing up in my rearview mirror, seeing them a little closer each time I did. Yes, it was Chief, I recognized the Jeep's headlights as his bigger engine slowly closed the distance between us.

We skidded to a stop in front of the house only seconds apart, the rogues cursing and setting the grass between us ablaze. All of us used various spells to dampen the fires and finally put them out. By the time we did, the rogues had vanished into the woods surrounding the house.

I glanced up at the slowly setting sun. Even if we hadn't shown up, the vampires would have risen soon, anyway.

I guess my plan works. Unless they start attacking in the morning...

I ran through the wards, my intent letting me pass right through, and knocked on the door. "It's me!"

The door cracked a little and Dennis' eye peeked through by the chain. "What's the password?"

"Hassenpfeffer," I said jokingly.

"That is correct." He closed the door and I heard the chain slide off before the door opened all the way.

"Got it on my first guess," I said and walked inside. "Everybody okay?"

"Nothing a nap won't fix," Alista said, sounding a little shaken.

"Great job, you two. Seriously."

Alista nodded and Dennis blushed. "Dot, I don't think either one of us could have done it by ourselves. There were nine of them all around the perimeter, attacking from all sides. We had to split up. Alista took the back and I took the front." Dennis looked at me concernedly.

"So, we need to have two people here is what you're telling me."

"Yes. Maybe a third to rotate."

"That's kind of brilliant. I'll take care of it right away. I wish we had more bedrooms," I said wistfully.

189

"We can use the garage. Some space heaters would be enough."

"I'll make it happen. You don't mind staying?"

He shook his head. "Not at all," he replied with a little smile. "But I do have to work tomorrow night…"

"Gotcha. I'll see if I can get you a replacement for then."

"Ask Dwight and Jason. They might do it."

"Especially since I'm now paying you all." I made a point to look over his shoulder at Alista. They both opened their mouths to object, and I held up my hand. "Don't wanna hear it. This isn't a volunteer service. Security details get paid. End of story."

"Yes, ma'am."

"I'll be out front. I think the others are searching the area. Holler when our friends wake up."

"I'm awake." Yuki said from her doorway.

"Good morning," I said with a smile.

"I'm guessing we had visitors?"

"A few actually. You seem to be quite popular."

"They just want me for my bod," she quipped, quite unruffled.

"I'm glad you're safe." I turned to the other two. "Call again if we're needed and get some rest. We'll feed the wards before we go."

"Thanks, Dot." Dennis gave me a quick hug.

"Miss Blackwell?"

"Dot, Yuki. Call me Dot."

"Sorry. Dot, thank you."

She bowed a little and slipped back into George's room.

A crack of thunder outside the house caused us all to jump. I raced out the front door to find Josie and Candace huddled together and no sign of Chief or Jimmy. "Where are they?"

"They're out back."

"Keep the wards fed," I said, but didn't feel any more attacks on them. "Fuck."

I raced around the outside of the house and saw a break through the trees. Leaving the shields, I ran through it and followed the unused trail leading deeper into the woods.

I kept walking, watching warily in every direction when the sound of voices led me to the right place. One of the rogues had been bound in Chief's spell, struggling futilely against them. He and Jason were standing over him and…arguing?

"Caught a rat?"

Chief nodded.

"So, what's the problem?"

"What to do with him," Jason answered.

"What did he say?"

"He doesn't speak English. Just some sort of Slavic."

"Anybody in the clan speak anything like that?"

"I do," Candace's meek voice came from behind me.

She and Josie had followed me into the woods. "I thought you were supposed to be feeding the shields?"

"We did. Then we came to find you," Josie answered.

"Can you unbind his mouth?"

Chief nodded at Josie and immediately a barrage of words I couldn't identify, let alone understand, came flying out. Candace concentrated on what he was saying and said something back.

The rogue stopped talking and narrowed his eyes at her.

They exchanged a few more words and she shook her head at me. "He won't tell us anything. Said he would rather die."

"Well that's not happening, either. I'll haul him into town and put him in a cell," Chief said determinedly.

"So he can work magic in front of humans? Scare the piss out of them? I'm telling you that's a bad idea, Bill." Jimmy said angrily.

"Well, what else do you want me to do. I'm not killing him!"

"Lady?" Jimmy was pleading with me.

I didn't see an option. "Bill. If Dane were here, holding him might be an option. You can't be there all the time."

"Are you ordering me to do it?"

"No. I'm asking you to step aside and let *me* do it. Not your job."

He stepped back without arguing, and I moved forward, not relishing what came next. Holding my hand above him I canted softly, "*Bheith ar dóiteáin!*"

He didn't even have time to scream. There was a flash of heat and a puff of smoke that burned my eyes and throat. Without a word, I turned and walked away, letting the rest of them deal with the charred remains.

I sat in my car and waited, not entirely comfortable with what I had done, even though I'd been left with little choice. It wasn't the first life I had taken, and I was sure it wouldn't be the last. It took only a few minutes for Chief to come out and head for my car.

I turned the key and rolled down the window, not cranking the engine. Putting my elbow on the ledge of the window, I waited to see how he would react to what I'd done.

He stopped and put his hand on my arm. "You all right?"

"Yeah. It had to be done."

"I know."

"Don't like taking lives, Chief?"

"No. I'll go the extra mile to avoid it, even in mundane situations. I even threw my gun at a bad guy's head once to avoid shooting him."

That made me laugh because I could picture it.

"Just sorry to make you do it."

"That's the difference. It *is* my job."

He nodded, knowing it was. "Doesn't make it easier."

I shook my head. "Why is killing witches different from killing humans? I've killed before, it's always harder if they're witches. Even rogue ones."

"Probably because it's closer to home. Gives us a sense of our own mortality. We could live forever, but often don't."

"Thanks, Bill."

He nodded and headed for his Jeep. I watched him as he backed up and spun around, heading off into the night. The rest of them showed up after and solemnly got into my car.

"I should probably tell them what happened before we leave," I said and opened my door.

"I did. Dennis came out." Jimmy gently closed my door.

I nodded at Jimmy, grateful for taking care of it. "Thanks."

"My pleasure. Thank you, too. He was being Chief again. Stubborn ass."

"He was doing what he thought right. He's fine. Let's grab some dinner and go home. Feels like a pizza and movie kind of night."

∞ ∞ ∞

"Candace, I need you to do something for me…"

Her eyes lit up eagerly.

"I need you to find out who owns the local blood bank. If it's a corporation, I need the managing member's name and anything else you can find. If it's a non-prof, I need to know all that information, too. Whatever you can find. I assume the hospital would be the best place to find it."

"Yes, Lady."

"Thank you." She went back to munching on her cheese pizza. We got two, one with and one without pepperoni. Josie was sharing the without with her. Jimmy and I were greedily gobbling up the other one between sips of beer.

With that portion of my ever-growing list of things to get done outsourced, I could focus on the other things. I went through my list of possible candidates and started making detailed notes of what I could remember about the people on my list. It wasn't as much as I thought it would be. The Coven of the Black Well was my mother's, I was just a member. I hadn't taken as much of an interest in everyone as I should have. Maybe I knew deep in my heart that I would never be their high priestess.

After the last slice was eaten, I cleaned up, grabbed my laptop and lay on my stomach in the middle of the bed. I navigated to Wally World's website and started perusing area rugs, single beds, and storage. If we needed more witches, they were going to need a place to sleep in the already over populated house. I'd make the garage as comfortable as possible. I even bought a couple of large space heaters.

"Whatcha doin'?" Jimmy flopped on the bed next to me.

"Buying beds and heaters and everything else to turn the garage into living quarters. They deliver, but it will take a week. I marked the order for pickup. Can I borrow your truck in the morning?"

"I can do you one better. I'll grab Dennis and go pick it up for you and drop it over at the house."

"You'd do that for little old me?"

"You betcha. Especially if you throw in a kiss as payment."

"Deal." I leaned over and kissed him.

"Such a deal," he whispered as I pulled away.

"I need more people."

"So, get some."

"Thinking about that now. Would you get all jealous if I flew back to Ashville with Chief for a day? I don't want to invite people to come live here if they're unsuitable. I figured if I take him along to the interviews, he can't bitch later."

"Have I mentioned how brilliant you are lately?"

"Seriously, you don't mind?"

He leaned in close and kissed me. "Not if you tell me about it when you get back. Seriously, I'm never going to bitch, so just stop asking. Just never keep anything from me is all I ask."

"Don't worry about that. It's too much fun telling you…"

He chuckled and kissed my shoulder.

"I wish you and Dennis didn't have to work all the time. With as much going on, I could use your help full time."

"Alas, there is rent to be paid, truck payments, cell phone bills, food…"

"I know."

"You know who might be a good candidate…"

"Who?"

"Jason."

"He works at the factory…"

"And how much do you think he makes at said factory?"

"Honestly, I don't have a clue."

"Try minimum wage. Dwight is shift supervisor, so he makes a bit more."

"You're kidding me."

"No. As I said, the economy sucks. People take what they can get. You might want to think about stealing Jason away from the factory to work in your bookstore. You could put him to work now and knock some little jobs off your list."

I rolled the idea around in my head. It could work. I hit the complete order button on my laptop and heard my phone ding with the confirmation email. After closing the lid, I pounced my brilliant boyfriend, crawling on top of him and kissing him all over his face.

"What will you do to me if I mention that you could probably talk Dwight into some part-time work watching the vampires?"

"Hmmm. Might take you into my mouth…"

"Ohhh. I need to be brilliant more often."

"Don't we all. Do you think he'd do it?"

He looked at his watch and frowned. "Their shift started an hour ago, or I'd say call them."

He was being too helpful with this and had that Jimmy gleam in his eye. "Wait."

"What?"

I narrowed my eyes at him and moved my face within inches of his. "Are you trying to set Jason up as my personal assistant to get me to fool around with him, too?"

He grinned. "I wasn't, but I kind of like that idea…"

"Seriously. Like I don't have enough to handle with you and Chief."

"You think he's hot."

"Well, yes, but…"

"Dot. I'm not and I wasn't. I'll just say, I wouldn't mind if it happened and leave it at that."

"Fine."

"Good."

He chuckled and flipped on his back, head on my pillow, stretching like a big sexy cat. I poked him in the stomach. "So, no matter how many boyfriends I could possibly end up with…you won't care?"

"Well, I'm sure there would be a limit. How about I promise to tell you if you get close?"

I stared at him incredulously. "You're insane."

"No. I just know how I feel about you, and I'm pretty sure I know how you feel about me. I'm not worried about anybody stealing you away from me."

"What about me? You do know that even thinking about you with another woman makes me growl. I'm *very* possessive."

"And do you think there is a single woman on this planet that could turn me on more than you? No, Dot. You can get as growly as you want. It will never happen."

"Promise?"

"I swear upon my soul and my life. I am yours."

That earned him a kiss and various other things. "Damn right you are. Be a shame to have to kill you dead."

He gave me a shit eating grin. "Not gonna happen anyway, so I'm not worried."

"What about if I was there?" I asked him out of curiosity, just to judge his reaction.

"Helping?"

"Yeah."

"Then she would be awfully bored. Because my attention would be focused solely on you. How could it not be?"

"You're fucking smooth."

"No, but I could be. Did you want to shave me? That might be fun."

"Is there no limit to your kinks?"

"I'll let you know." He gave me a mischievous grin.

"Do you have your phone?"

I nodded. "With all the shit happening at the other house, I'm afraid to set it down." I grabbed it off the bed.

"May I see it?"

"Want to see my texts?"

"Nope."

I shot him a suspicious glance but handed it to him. If he could trust me, I could trust him. A little.

He took it from me and got up off the bed. "Pay attention to the computer. Pretend you're looking at porn. Better yet, put some porn on it."

"Okay?" I opened a new incognito browser and opened the site I used every once in a great while.

He moved to behind me and took a step over, clicking the shutter button on the phone. He reached above him and

197

pulled the light chain on the ceiling fan. "That's better." He took the same picture again, but a little lower.

"What are you doing?"

"You'll see."

He stepped a little closer, lifted my shirt above my waist, and straddled my thighs. I heard the shutter button again. He scooted back a little and reached up, tugging my leggings over my ass. *Click.* He got up again, tugged them down to my ankles, and moved over by the dresser.

"Put your right arm under you and tilt your head back."

"Like I'm touching myself?"

"Exactly."

I rolled my eyes and did as he asked.

He reached over, grabbing my pants and tugging them the rest of the way off. "Would you spread your legs?"

I did it, my thong clearly visible.

"Wow. That's hot. Put your finger on it where I can see it."

I did. *Click.*

He set the phone down and reached up, tugging my panties down just below my ass. I hated to admit it, but I was getting *really* turned on just from being photographed.

"Okay, now reach down a little lower and slip your finger inside, just a little."

I didn't have to be asked twice. A tiny moan escaped my lips. *Click.*

"Okay. That's good enough."

"For what?" I rolled over and gasped, Candace was in my doorway. I pulled my panties up.

My phone made the *woop* sending noise.

"Jimmy. What did you do with those pictures?" Staring at him incredulously, I forgot about Candace altogether.

He handed me my phone. I opened my messages and saw he had sent every single one of them to Chief.

"Now we wait," he said as he lay on the bed.

"For what?"

"Twenty bucks says he sends you a picture of his dick."

"What? No way. You're on," I laughed. He didn't know Mr. Boy Scout like I did.

My phone *bleeped.*

Confidently, I opened the messaging app back up. "Ha!" I turned my phone to Jimmy and showed him his one-line response.

Woah. You are gorgeous.

"Pay up, bitch!"

"Wait for it," he whispered with a smile.

"It's not going to happen."

"I say it will."

"This is *Chief* we're talking about. The only thing he'd send a picture of is his Jeep."

The phone was still pointed at Jimmy when it went *bleep* again. His expression didn't change so I figured he sent a thank you or something equally as innocuous. I turned the screen to see what he sent and saw a picture of his very erect manhood being squeezed by his fist.

"Son of a bitch."

Jimmy started laughing with no signs of stopping. Even Candace was giggling in the doorway.

I can never win. I'm not betting anymore. Ever.

"How did you know?"

"I told him I would give him ten bucks to send you a dick pic later. He would know when."

"You have got to be kidding me! You cheated?"

"No. I just thought it would be funny to tell you I did. He's a *guy*, Dot. If you send nude pictures of yourself to any man, you will get pictures in return. It's like engrained into our DNA."

"You're so full of shit."

"Want to test this theory?"

"Uh… Yeah. Not so much. I'll trust you."

"Bout damn time."

CHAPTER 18

The new Keurig worked awesomely, and I didn't have to threaten it once to hurry up. It was my reward for it taking me thirteen minutes to figure out how to use it. I grabbed my steamy mug of happiness and took a sip.

"Mmmm."

Candace walked out of my bedroom, sleepy eyed. I really needed to buy her scuffy-footed pajamas. The ones with plastic-bottomed feet built into them that made *scuff scuff* noises when you walked.

She'd be adorable. Adorabler? Whatever.

With eyes closed and one handed, she popped the brewer open, flipped out the pod, grabbed another and shoved it in like she was loading the magazine into a Glock, slammed the lid shut, and hit brew. Before it even started, she grabbed a mug out of the cabinet and had it underneath it.

"That was the most amazing fucking thing I've ever seen. You're like a damn coffee ninja. How did you do that without looking?"

"We have one at work. I need it to live. It became necessary to master it."

"Teach me, *sensei*."

"You are not ready, grasshopper."

I bowed my head in defeat, vowing to train myself to one day be worthy.

She leaned forward and wrapped her arms around my stomach, hugging me. I still had trouble believing how short she stood. If she was five-feet it would have been a miracle. I'd say four-ten, four-eleven max. If it weren't for her obvious feminine charms, people would probably mistake her for a teenager. I bet she *did* get carded a lot.

I petted her head absentmindedly, until her coffee started gurgling and was done. She let go of me like yesterday's newspaper and scooped it up, sniffed it repeatedly making animalistic noises, and took a sip.

"That's the good shit."

I think that might have been the first time I ever heard her swear. "Watch your language, young lady."

"Yes, Mom."

We both laughed and clinked mugs.

I grabbed my phone off the counter and walked over to the couch, sitting down with one leg underneath me. Candace sat across from me, eyeing the seat next to me, though. I patted it and she immediately got up and moved.

"You know you don't have to be so afraid. If you want to sit somewhere in this house, next to me, next to Josie, wherever. You sit where you want to sit. Like the grocery store. I saw you eyeballing the mint hot cocoa. If you wanted it, why didn't you ask?"

"Four hundred years of being beaten if I asked for water."

Yep. That would do it.

"Candace, I apologize. I didn't think of that."

"It's okay. Another lifetime."

I wrapped my arm around her and pulled her close, kissing the top of her head. "Next time you feel like that, remember…if it would make you happy, I would do it in a heartbeat."

She blushed and nodded, setting her mug down on the table and standing up. She reached down and pulled my leg out from beneath me and sat on my lap, laying back against me.

"You said I could sit anywhere I wanted, right?"

202

I chuckled and wrapped my arms around her. "Yep. But you need to hand me my coffee." She reached over and grabbed my mug by the rim, offering me the handle. I sat there and drank my coffee holding a woman six-hundred years my senior like a kid.

Josie walked out of the room and plopped down on the loveseat across from us, smiling softly.

"Morning," Candace said and gave her a smile.

"Sucking up to Dot, I see."

Candace nodded, and her smile morphed into a grin. Josie laughed and rolled her eyes. "Do you want coffee?"

"Yes, but stay where you are, I'll get it."

I'd known Josie, literally, my entire life. I'd seen firsthand how jealous she got. For the life of me, I couldn't fathom why she didn't feel like that when Candace got clingy with me. Then again, there was nothing normal about *any* of my personal relationships.

"I still don't get it," I said aloud.

"What?"

"Nothing."

"Ask Josie if she wants to sit in your lap."

"Uh, she's a perv. She'd sit on my face if I'd let her."

Candace let out a musical giggle. "Ask her, though. See if she has the desire."

She was trying to make a point that I wasn't getting. I waited a minute for her to bring her mug of coffee into the living room and sit back down. When she finally did, I asked her. "Hey Josie, want to sit in my lap?"

"Can I?" She set the mug down.

"Um." I looked down at Candace. "Can she?"

Candace smiled knowingly, nodded, and scooted over to the couch seat next to me. As soon as she moved, Josie got up and came over, sitting down on my lap and leaning back against me, sighing contentedly. She didn't fit nearly as well as Candace, but seemed perfectly content.

You could hear my neck creak as I slowly turned my head to the little witch next to me. "Did you cast a spell on her or something?"

She laughed, shaking her head. "No. You did."

"Excuse me?"

"Think about it."

I tried. I even had trouble drawing a blank. I couldn't figure anything out. "I don't get it. What's going on?"

"You are our Lady."

"*Candace*… I know I'm your high priestess, what the hell does that have to do with anything?"

"Your mother has multiple lovers, doesn't she?"

"Yeah. She's freaky."

"Those in houses of glass…"

"Yeah, yeah. What of it?"

She sighed, almost impatiently. "Most high priestesses are simply place holders for those the goddess bless as *true* high priestesses. We are not mortal, our birthrates are low. We can not conceive unless we *choose* to. True high priestesses are like queens of the hive. We are drawn to her, to protect her, love her, and the chosen few, *mate* with her."

"What?"

"She says you're queen bee. I tried to explain it to you before, but you just shrugged it off."

"What?"

Even Josie rolled her eyes.

"So, these feelings of love, aren't your own?" The thought kind of turned my stomach but explained a whole lot of shit.

"Absolutely they are. We can hate you and leave you, but I'll be honest. I want to be near you or touch you all the time," Josie said straight faced.

"Do you find me more attractive?"

"I've always thought you were hot, but no. No more than usual."

"That's a relief. Wait, do you both have the urge to mate with me?"

They both nodded.

"Too bad."

Candace laughed. Josie looked hurt.

"This is just too weird for words. This is why nobody is getting as jealous as they should be?"

"Yes. We're all just happy to be with you."

"Is there a way to stop it and why do you know so much about it," I eyeballed her suspiciously.

"No. And I was purchased by a true high priestess. It was she that set me free and explained what I was. I didn't even know I was a witch. My previous masters thought I was just fae."

That made a lot of sense. I ruffled her hair. "Thank you for telling me. Why did you wait so long?"

"I was not sure until a few days ago, and then I was not certain you would welcome the news. Until I saw you struggling with not knowing."

"It's been bothering the shit out of me. Between Bill, Jimmy, Josie, and you, I thought there was something in the water."

"I'm sure you will draw more to your side. I will pass along the warning I was told. It is a heady power. Do not abuse the gift of the goddess. It will drive those that you love away."

I wasn't worried about me. I was worried about those around me, Especially Jimmy. He had a tendency to go a little overboard. Maybe a lot.

I put my hand on her knee. "Thank you. I don't think you have to worry about that."

"I know. You are a great woman, Dorothea."

"Dot."

"It would have sounded funny, and not imposed my meaning, if I said Dot."

"Well, I need to get moving. I need to find Jason and Dwight."

"Why?" Josie sounded curious.

"Going to see if they want to work for me."

"Um. Okay? Pool boys without a pool?"

"I wouldn't mind seeing Jason in a speedo. Dwight not so much." The thought of the ultra-thin, balding conspiracy theorist made me want to turn to a life of celibacy. He was strange, even for a witch. "What are your plans for the day?"

"Want to wander around town, sweets?" Josie asked her girlfriend.

"Sweets?" I couldn't help but ask.

"Yep. Sweets. Candy. Nomnoms."

"Remind me never to ask about any of your other pet names."

"I would like that, honey pot." Candace replied with an evil grin, answering Josie but staring at me.

"Ew." I pushed Josie off my lap and ignored her fit of giggles.

∞ ∞ ∞

I dropped Josie and Candace off in town and spun around, heading for Farrell's motel. I parked next to Bessie, got out, and knocked on Number Two. It took a moment for the door to open and a sleepy looking Jason peeked out through the chained door.

"Dot?"

"In the flesh."

The door closed and opened without the chain.

"Everything okay?"

"Mostly. Dwight here?"

Jason nodded, stepping back and pointing at the lump under the covers in the other bed.

"Good. Got a minute? Want to talk to you both."

"Dwight!" He reached over and grabbed a pillow off his bed, launching it at Dwight's feet. "Wake up."

The covers lifted off his feet exposing his head. He slept on the bed upside down for some reason known only to him. I didn't want to know why.

"What? Oh. Hi, Lady."

I nodded at him. He wrapped the comforter around him and got up, heading for the bathroom and grabbing his clothes off the floor.

"He's going to get dressed," Jason told me.

"I figured." *Thank the goddess.*

"Sit?" He pointed at his bed.

"No, I'm okay. You look tired, sorry for waking you early."

"That's okay."

He wore a pair of boxers, blue and red pinstriped, and nothing else. I found myself staring at his abs and wondering how hard they would feel under my fingertips.

"Um, Lady. My eyes are up here..." He pointed at his face.

"Sorry!" I flushed. "Was just wondering how many sit-ups you do a day."

He laughed. "A lot. And I run a lot, squats, pullups. Not a lot to do in the middle of the woods and I need to stop the beer from collecting in the middle."

"It's working."

"Thanks."

Thankfully the bathroom door opened back up and Dwight came out in jeans and a T-shirt. "Sorry, Lady. What can we do for you?"

"Dwight, I understand you're shift manager at the factory?"

He nodded.

"Would you like to make some extra cash during the day?"

"Doing?"

"Feeding the wards in case the vampires are attacked again?"

"Again?" They both asked in unison.

"Yes. Yesterday. Dennis and Alista, a witch from my home town, kept them at bay. We caught one of them, but the rest got away."

"Where is he?"

I shook my head.

He smiled at that. "I'd love to. I can always use some extra cash."

"Dennis and Jimmy picked up furniture and stuff for a bunk room over there. I'll also pay you and Jason to go put all the furniture and things together."

"You game, kid?"

"Hell yeah." They even fist-bumped. It was cute and creepy.

"Good. Thank you, Dwight."

"You want us to head over there now?"

"In a minute. Can I speak to you outside for a minute, Dwight?"

He nodded but looked unsure.

I didn't elaborate, just turned and walked outside, ignoring a confused Jason.

Dwight pulled the door shut behind him. "Everything okay?"

"Yes. I want to steal Jason from the factory. I've heard how much he makes an hour."

He actually smiled at me. "Please do. Kid's smart as shit. He's wasted in the factory, but I couldn't do anything to help him."

I sighed in relief. Dwight was many things, including a good friend to Jason. "Thank you. I have a ton of shit going on and I need help. Our coven is also likely to be growing very soon and there will be mountains of things to coordinate."

"How much bigger?"

"More than double. Are you okay with that?"

"Any lookers?"

I laughed. "Yes. A few."

"All for it!"

I hugged him and motioned for the door. He opened it back up and strode in, kind of strutting a little. I shook my head and looked everywhere but at him. At least I could take satisfaction in the fact that he seemed genuinely happy for his young friend. Sighing, I walked back in.

"Want to come work for me full time?"

Jason blinked a couple of times. "What?"

I told him exactly what I told Dwight. His eyes lit up at the thought of the coven growing but seemed a little worried about something. "What?"

"I'd love to, but I can't leave Dwight alone in that hell hole."

"Hey, kid."

Jason turned to Dwight.

"I caught you smoking pot last night," he lied. "I'm sorry, I'm going to have to fire you."

"What? You did not. Shut up, old man."

"Did, too. You can smell it on him, right, Dot?"

I immediately saw what he was doing. Playing along, I leaned forward and took a whiff. He smelled *good*. "Yep. Smells like marijuana to me, Shift Supervisor Dwight, sir."

"Now I have a witness. Come pick up your check on Friday."

"Do you random drug test your employees, Dot?" Jason asked, jokingly.

"Nope," I said, stifling my laughter.

"Whew. Okay then. I accept. Thank you both."

"Don't talk to me, reefer addict." Dwight gave him a shunning look.

CHAPTER 19

Jason and I walked into the diner. I waved to Marge and slipped into my table. Jason started laughing quietly. I gave him a curious look and he pointed to the edge of the table by the window. There was an engraved plastic sign on it.

Reserved for Dot

I looked up at the kitchen window and Herb was staring at me, silently laughing. Marge took my picture holding the sign. I shook my head and blew them both a kiss.

"Now *that's* funny," Jason said, still chuckling.

"Only cuz you're on drugs."

"You know I don't really smoke pot, right?"

That revelation kind of shocked me. "Really?"

"I've tried it, but not a huge fan."

"Huh. You haven't smoked it, got naked with Josie, and watched Disney movies."

His eyebrows rose. "Can I?"

"No." Jealousy gripped my stomach, threatening my appetite. *What the fuck? Him, too?*

"Damnit." He winked to let me know he was kidding. I wished he would tell the little green monster inside me.

Marge walked up to us. "Whatcha guys want to drink?"

"Coffee and coke."

"Just coffee."

"Like the nameplate? Herb got the biggest kick out of having that made."

"I bet he did. Why?"

"Your damn sandwich. We've had people we haven't seen in years coming in to order it. Biggest way to get something to spread is to tell them it's a secret menu item. People come in to see if it's real."

"What is?"

I looked over at Jason. "Herb named a sandwich after me."

"I'll have that," he said, setting his menu down.

"You don't even know what's in it."

"I don't care. It has to be delicious."

I blushed and turned my attention to the menu. I wanted meat, not sweet. "I'll have a burger, well, with fries."

Marge nodded, grabbed the menus, and headed off to fill our drinks.

"Herb, one Dotwhich and a cow patty, well."

"She knows you're a witch?"

"Pretty sure she meant the witch in sandwich…"

"Oh."

"So, what do you want me to do first?"

"Relax. Work starts after meal. I'll drop you off by Dwight and you guys can follow me over to the new house."

"I can't believe you bought another one."

"Mine's too small to fit everybody."

"They're nice?"

He didn't say the V-word, but I knew who he meant. I nodded. "They're just people."

"Undead ones…"

"Shhh. You'll see."

"So, get the garage room put together?"

"Yes. And introduce yourselves to Alista. She's volunteering right now but moving here soon with her brother. They own a bakery and are going to open one here."

"That's kind of awesome."

She grinned. "It is. Also, pick up a notebook to write all this stuff down in. I'm a scatterbrain and totally unorganized. Speak up if I forget stuff and keep me out of trouble."

"Yes, Lady."

"None of that shit. I'm still just Dot."

"There's no such thing as just Dot."

"Oh, you little sweet talker you. It's your first day and I don't give out raises until you've proven your worth."

He blushed. "That wasn't a compliment, it was the truth."

"Okay, put yourself down for a quarter an hour raise."

"You haven't even told me how much I'm going to be making…"

"How much did you make at the factory?"

"About eleven an hour…"

"Are you fucking kidding me?"

"No. It's supposed to go up to almost twelve at the end of next month."

"You're finally getting a raise?"

"No. Minimum wage is going up."

I shook my head. "How much do you want?"

He looked everywhere but at my eyes. I used the moment to study his angular face. He really was beautiful, all the angles made him seem a little cold, but the blue of his eyes rounded it out a little.

Yep. Hot.

"Would fourteen be too much to ask for?"

"Let's round it up to twenty. Welcome to First Moon Enterprises," I reached out my hand to shake on it, but he stared at me.

"You can't pay me that much, Lady."

"I can do whatever the hell I want."

"But that's insane. Dwight doesn't even make that much. Not even close."

"He does when he does work for me. Starting wage."

He looked around the diner. "How rich are you?" His voice had become a whisper. I'd never been comfortable talking about money, but if he needed reassurance…

"My own or family money?"

"You have both?"

"I'm a hundred years old. I started investing when I was ten. I bought some *very* lucrative stocks. I could live on the dividends alone, they have doubled so many times. I've bought an insane amount of stock in a shit ton of startup companies that are the major corporations of today. And that's just my bank account. My family is *ancient*. Do the math, Jason."

His eyes blinked rapidly.

"That stays between us. People treat you differently when they find out you can buy a small country. I splurge, but not insanely. I bank behind the scenes and hide most of my money. I'm only telling you all this because I'm going to give you access to some of these accounts to make purchases for the new bookstore and other things that I'll let you in on when the time comes, okay?"

He nodded in shock.

"Enough about money. Welcome to the team."

"Thanks?"

Chief walked into the diner and blinked when he saw me sitting with Jason. "Got him out of bed? You are a miracle worker."

"Bill, meet my new assistant, Jason. Jason, this is Bill."

"Assistant?"

"Yes. I've got too much going on and need help. Dwight also works for me now, part-time."

"Wait. You don't work at the factory anymore?"

"No. I got fired."

"Why?"

"So I could go work for Dot."

"Dwight was okay with that?"

"He practically kicked me out the door."

"Good. You hated that place." Chief even patted him on the back.

"Keep an eye on her, though. Let me know if she's doing anything illegal."

"I'm sorry, officer. If you wish to investigate my client, you're going to need a warrant."

"See? I hired the right guy." I slid in and let him sit down next to me. I rubbed his leg as soon as he was close enough.

"Hi, Lady." He leaned over and stole a kiss.

"Hey yourself, sexy sheriff."

"Chief."

"Cheeky Chief." It was corny, but I reached under him and squeezed his butt, kind of. Mostly his wallet.

He rolled his eyes, but I saw the start of a smile in the corner of his mouth. "So, I'm assuming ward feeding has been taken care of?"

"Yep. Dwight shall be spending days there, and Jason if he has time. I'd like a couple more but that won't happen until we bring in some more of us. Speaking of which, I'd like to expedite that. Do you have any vacation time?"

"Uh. I don't think I've taken a day off in a couple of years. So, yes. Why?"

"I want to do some interviews."

"I need to take time off to do this?"

"Yes. As we will be conducting them in Ashville."

"Wait, what?"

"Well, do you expect me to make them come all the way out here and if we don't like them, send them packing?"

"I see your point."

"I knew you would. When do you want to go?"

"Is there nobody on the list you can shortlist? Maybe get them out here soon? I'll trust your judgement and then we can interview the rest after thanksgiving. Second week of December?"

"Assistant, put that in my calendar, and book the sheriff and I a flight, please."

"Wait. You're serious?"

"No. Well, kinda, but I need to get you a bank card and show you how to– Nevermind. Don't panic."

He breathed a sigh of relief.

"Did you see your sign?"

I rolled my eyes at Chief. "Yes."

"I saw it yesterday and laughed."

Marge brought the food over and set a double burger and fries in front of Chief. "I'll bring your coke in a second."

"Thanks, Marge."

I took a bite of my burger while I watched Jason taste his. He stopped chewing and stared at me. "You're delicious."

It's a good thing she hadn't brought Chief his coke yet. He would have spit it everywhere.

I blushed and rushed to change the subject. "So, everybody keeps calling it the factory. What is it they make?"

Jason laughed. "Want to take a guess?"

"Dildos?"

"Close. The other thing that gives ecstasy to women. Ice cream scoops."

"True story." My phone began ringing on the table next to me. It was Josie probably wondering where I was. "Jello," I answered.

"Dot…they took her…Candace," she said between sobs.

∞ ∞ ∞

I rocked Josie back and forth on the couch in the vampires' home. She'd been beaten, bloody, and hysterical when we got to where they'd left her. It took nearly ten minutes to get the story out of her.

One of them knew how to drive. Josie and Candace had been walking along Main when a white van pulled over, and seven of them jumped out casting binding spells, much to the dismay of the other pedestrians. They tossed them in the van and drove away, not stopping anywhere. They knocked Josie unconscious, stuffed a note in her mouth, and dumped her in an alleyway.

The note was very clear.

House of wards before dark. Give us vampires.

They wanted to exchange Candace for the vampires.

I loved her, but it wasn't going to happen. The coven, and I mean all of us, had gathered inside the house where our new friends slept. The house I'd worked so hard on to make a safe haven for them. All to be undone by a single kidnapping.

"You sure they'll have her with them?" Josie asked for the thirteenth time.

"They have to. There's no way we'd turn over the vampires without her," Chief answered levelly, no emotion coloring his words.

"Supposedly. It's not happening," I said angrily.

"You're not going to save her?" The tears on her cheeks and the fear in her voice broke my heart.

"I didn't say that. I said I wasn't going to sacrifice the vampires for her."

"What's the plan, Lady?"

The chief of police had just asked me how we were going to save her. I didn't have the heart to say I didn't know. "I need a minute alone to think. Jimmy, take Josie for me."

I got up and he slid into my spot on the couch. The coven watched as I walked out the front door without a jacket and walked into the middle of the yard, dropped to my knees, and prayed. I prayed to our goddess to keep our friend safe. We'd lost too many already. Candace was one that could never be replaced.

"All of you are precious to me."

Shivers ran down my arms as I recognized the voice, the voice that had spoken to me from my body. I couldn't open my eyes. My fear keeping them shut. I could feel her all around me.

"They are to me, too. How do I save the one?" The tears began rolling down my cheeks and the sobs crawled from my chest. "I can't lose her."

"Do what is right, that is all you can. Remember that death is not the end. The fae child knows this and is not afraid."

"There is no way to save her?" My chest froze and I couldn't breathe past the lump in my throat.

"That, I did not say. The possibilities are endless. When the moment comes, you will know what needs to be done. Have faith, not in me, but in yourself, child. I chose you and have placed *my* faith in you."

Eyes still closed, I nodded. "Thank thee, Lady."

Her lips touched the invisible mark on my forehead, the mark she had put there with those same lips, warm and cold, hard and soft. Fingers slipped through my hair, pulling it from my face and a moment later she was gone, leaving me shivering in the cold.

But she had left me with something else. Determination.

I pulled my knees from the muck the melting snow had left in the yard, standing and turning to see my family in the window. I went back inside. Not one of them spoke as they all knelt on the floor.

"I need four volunteers. Two women and two men."

Josie was the first to stand, as did Alista. Poor Alista, who had come all this way to set a trap and put herself in danger. Jimmy and Dennis stood just after. I gave them a small smile. They'd told the battalion chief a friend had been kidnapped, a tale he could corroborate with the chief of police if he needed.

I had the bait, now the trap needed to be set.

218

We rushed, gathering what we could and making due without. I'd vainly attempted to wake Yuki. Sunset was still too far away and even knocking on the stone window of the bedroom hadn't done any good. Those were their tombs and they were dead to the world. I would not bust down the door. Ever.

The garage was the stage.

When we were complete, I walked outside and pulled down all the wards and shields myself, inviting the rogues to come and play.

CHAPTER 20

I waited in front of the garage door by myself, trusting everybody not to move. Josie, bandaged, stood in the front window watching me and hoping. The first of them peeked from the woods on the side of the house opposite from where I stood. I did nothing to spook him, no movement, not even a breath.

He nodded across the way and another stepped out from the side closest to me, raised his hand, and let a blast of sparks fly into the air above us. I wondered who he had signaled when the white van skidded to a stop in front of the house, rocking before the side door slid open with a screech of metal. Six more rogues poured out of the van, taking up positions in front of the house, arms out, ready to cast.

Then I saw her, kneeling in the van and bound in rope. Candace with a knife to her throat. One last heavily hooded rogue sat on a milk crate beside her. The insurance.

"You have them, yes?" His voice practically echoed from the van. He had to have been using magic to make himself heard without shouting. His voice dripped with a heavy accent. At least I could understand him. I knew one of them spoke English. The note was proof of that.

"Yes. Behind this door." I shouted so he could hear.

"Covered, *da*?" Panic seeped into his voice. He didn't want his precious treasures turning to dust if the door opened.

"Yes. I covered them with wool."

"Let me see."

Instead of opening the door, I held up my phone. "Look."

He nodded to the rogue closest to me. He scrambled over, fearful I was going to attack him, and grabbed the phone from my hand. He looked at it and ran it to the figure in the van.

He reached out a clawed hand and took it from him, holding it in front of the hood covering his head. Whatever he'd been at one time, he wasn't a witch anymore. His claws were proof of that. The feasibility of my plan became shrouded in doubt.

Fuck.

He tucked my phone into his pocket. I'd written it off as a loss the moment I'd given it up.

"Bring them to me."

"Not until you let her go."

He snarled under the hood and it slithered over my skin like an oily serpent. I fought the urge to rub my arms.

"Give them or dead she is."

"Compromise. I'll open the door but stand my ground. You let her go and I walk away. Their lives aren't worth the life of my daughter." I hoped he bought it.

The hood shifted as he looked down at Candace and then back up at me, chuckling. "Kin. Good." He pulled the blade to her throat and I watched as she winced, the blade creating an indent on her flesh, but not cutting in. Yet. "*Da.* Open the door."

I pulled the opener out of my pocket and held it above me, pressing the button. The motor whirred to life as the screw slowly lifted the heavy wooden door. He leaned forward and stared until the four bodies draped in heavy woolen black blankets came into view.

The hood tilted as he stared in uncertainty. "Proof."

I sighed, trying my best to look inconvenienced. It wasn't as hard as I would have thought. I'd been inconvenienced quite a few times over the past month. I had plenty of practice to nail the look.

I turned around and marched over to the body closest to me. I stood to the side and slowly peeled back the blanket, revealing the naked foot of one of the "vampires" lying in the bed while I whispered, "*Deataigh.*"

Smoke began to pour from the flesh and I quickly covered the foot before releasing the spell. I waved my hand in front of my face to clear my vision. I even coughed a little for effect.

"Others?"

"I assumed you meant alone. My friend is there in the window." I turned and pointed at Josie. She stared inside the van at the bound Candace, nearly pounding on the glass.

"Good. *Nogalini viṇu.*"

This should be the part where the trade goes sour and I show my resolve…

The rogue closest to me rushed forward to grab me, the words of a spell on his lips. His temple exploded as the shot from the rifle bored through his skull, dropping him like a stone on the driveway.

"I'm sorry, I meant to say me, her, and my friend with the well concealed rifle in case you tried to be a dick."

The other rogues looked at each other and then toward Chief, concealed somewhere in the trees.

Laughter erupted inside the van as the knife bobbed perilously against Candace's skin. If he didn't reign in his chuckles, he was going to accidentally slice her open.

He waved at the rogue who had delivered the cell phone. One handed, he picked Candace up by her bindings and gave her to him, along with the knife, before sitting down on the milk crate and putting his elbows on his knees to watch the exchange.

The rogue holding Candace walked forward, holding her against his chest with one arm and the knife in the other. I put my hands down by my sides and waited patiently for him to bring her to me. When he got closer than he liked, he stopped, setting her slowly to the ground.

I held my breath as he brought the knife to the rope around her ankles and quickly sawed through it, allowing her to walk.

"Candace, come here, honey." *Walk, baby. Just walk.*

She took one step and I reached out my hand. As soon as my fingers touched her, I pulled her to my chest and hugged her, backing us up slowly away from the garage.

"*Nest tos!*"

The rogues slowly walked forward. One step for each one of mine, eyes on the trees watching for danger. I stopped at the edge of the property, looking as innocent as I could. That should have been their first warning. I concentrated on picturing the cell phone in the bad guy's pocket and the cleverly placed combustion spell I had layered on the battery… "*Pléascadh.*"

The explosion was bigger than I expected from a cell phone. I remembered the headline news from a couple of years ago, banning people from travelling with a certain model. Any phone could be a bomb with the right spell. The concussion blew him from his egg crate into the back door of the van. I think it might have blown a good portion of his leg off, too.

I pushed Candace toward the back of the house, where Josie was running to meet her and get her to safety. The four "vampires" sat up in their beds and began casting incendiary explosions on the front lawn, causing the shotgun shells we'd placed tip-up in the ground to explode. Most didn't go off, but the few that did were spectacular. I watched as one of the rogues was shredded and another completely lost his arm. The repeated rapid-fire spells caused enough confusion and harm to the shielded rogues that the rest of my coven was able to walk forward on the roof where they'd been hiding and barrage them with binding spells. The rogues quickly became bound, gagged, and dropped to the ground.

We'd done it. And saved Candace.

The other's dropped to the ground from the roof, using their magic to slow them down. Dwight, Jason, and Jimmy had offered to dispatch any that remained alive and they held true to their word. They would never trouble us again.

I walked toward the van to check on the asshole who caused all this. Peeking my head in through the door. I screamed as a clawed hand shot out and grabbed me by the throat, dragging me into the darkness of the van.

He forgot his English, cursing at me in whatever language was his native. I endured the hissing and spittle, but when I saw his face I screamed. He was the stuff of nightmares. Long fangs protruded from his mouth and slit pupils nearly burned me in hatred as his forked tongue hung limply from the side of his mouth. Long pointed ears rose above his matted black hair, lightening into scales before becoming pale white flesh. Just from the touch of the skin on his hand I could feel four beings within him fighting for dominance.

He'd been a witch once. Until he came across a vampire in his village in Latvia. Wanting more power, he experimented, using his magic and the vampire's blood to change him. Then he came across a *smok* in some caverns in the mountains. At first, he thought it was just an extraordinary long snake until it turned into a dragon. He hired the witches with him today to help catch it. It died in the capture, but he still used its blood. Dead blood that mingled with the necromancy of the vampire blood already flowing through his veins. Many years later, he came across the elven maiden. She had been so sweet as he experimented with her. But her blood had been too pure and drove the three creatures living in his body insane.

"You're a monster," I managed to croak.

"*Da*," he hissed as his fangs tore into my neck. He needed my blood to heal, but in feeding, he'd exposed his head. The thunder of the Chief's sidearm blasted through the inside of the metal box I'd been trapped in a split second after his forehead exploded against the metal doors behind him.

I probably would have screamed if I weren't already dying from the poison burning through my flesh.

CHAPTER 21

"You did well, daughter. I could not have been more proud."

I glanced up at the loving face of the goddess standing over me, smiled, and inhaled the sweet scent of the flowers all around me. The sun warmed the hill I'd been nestled upon. "Not that well. I did die at the end."

"True, but death is only the beginning. I told you that."

I nodded, heartened by her kind words. "I'll miss them, though."

"Not for long."

I sat up in a panic. "No. They can't die! We worked so hard to save her, all of them. They were supposed to be happy."

She chuckled, sending the motes of sunlight playing on my arms dancing. "Silly, child. They're not dying, you're going back. Ten witches are fervently working to save you. It looks like it is working now that the vampires have drained the poison from your veins."

"Oh, good. I wanted to go back. I'm not ready yet."

"I know. You have much to do."

"Will I do it? Will my work pay off?"

"That depends on you. Don't give up and you will see it through."

"I will, my lady." I bowed my head and when I lifted it, I was sitting up in the middle of the garage, gasping for breath and wishing I was still dead. Until I saw the faces of everyone around me. Josie was a sobbing mess. With every wracking wail, my chest hurt a little more. Candace was holding her, tears running down her red cheeks. Jimmy, my poor Jimmy, had to be restrained by Dennis, he looked like he was going to kill something. Everyone else was crying and on their knees, not wanting to lose another high priestess again. And then their was Chief…

"Thank fuck," Chief said and dropped to the floor beside my bed. "Lady, damn it, Dot. Will you stop *doing* that?" He sounded angry, but I could hear the fear in his voice. He'd already lost one woman he loved and had been forced to face the possibility of losing another.

"What?"

"Dying!"

"I'll try. No promises."

"What the hell was that thing?" Jimmy asked as Dennis let him go, color returning to his pale complexion.

"I saw it. I saw it all. He was a corruption. You wouldn't believe the evil things he did." I shuddered with his memories still oozing through my head. I don't know how I saw it, but I think it had something to do with the goddess. She might have showed me as a warning. Not that I'd ever eat a snake, vampire, or elf.

"He smelled like an elf," Candace said, still stroking Josie's hair.

"You okay, sweetie?"

She nodded, but still looked pale.

"Am I okay?" I asked everyone. They all gave me a look.

"You have quite the scar where he bit you…" Jimmy said sadly.

"Let me see."

Josie leaned forward and took a picture with her phone before handing it to me. I glanced at the screen. The flesh around the wound had a green tinge to it. The actual *wounds* started at the top of my shoulder at the junction of my neck. When Chief shot him, the impact ripped the fangs down along my collar bone before they faded into two white lines. I shrugged. It could have been oh so much worse.

Battle wounds.

More like stupid wounds. You got bit because you were careless, stupid.

At least I had the sense to mentally berate myself. I had been stupid, thinking the creature was dead when I stuck my head in the door. I should have just set fire to the van to make sure and called it a day.

"Can we go home now? I feel gross."

"Can you even stand?" Chief sounded doubtful.

"If there's a shower involved, I could probably run right now." I rolled over and tried to sit up. It didn't work out so well. The after effects of the poison still lingering. "Okay, maybe not."

Yuki surprised me by kneeling in front of me. She bowed her head and smiled at me. "You were not joking when you said you are not like your mother. I just wanted to say thank you for saving us, once again."

"Team effort," I said, slowly reaching over and patting her head. "Thank all of you for getting the poison out of my system. If you and George stay, I hope this is the start of a long and prosperous friendship."

She nodded and stood. "Thank Yvette. She was the one who pulled the poison from you." She paused and looked around her. "Would you all please excuse us for a moment? I need to speak to your high priestess in private."

Everybody but Chief nodded, heading inside. He cocked an eyebrow at me. I nodded slowly so my head didn't spin. I doubted Yuki would be impressed if I puked on her shoes.

"Holler if you need me," Chief grumbled and headed inside.

Once the door leading to the house closed, Yuki leaned closer. "I would offer you blood to repay our debt."

"What?"

"The poison has been removed from your body, but it's effects remain. The damage was considerable. You will live, but not as strong as you were. I would like to give you my blood to drink."

"You want to turn me into a vampire?"

She stifled a giggle. "No. It will merely heal you. Turning someone into one of us is a little more…complicated. I do not even think it would work on a witch. That abomination," she paused to point at the van, "is what I think would happen if we tried."

"Oh, good. I like the sun too much."

A sad look passed over her face. "There is much to give up to live forever."

"I'm sorry, Yuki."

She shook her head. "I do not regret being what I am. I was born a vampire. Some of us had it forced upon us. It is they who deserve our pity."

I nodded, even though I couldn't imagine being forced into a new life. I'd been born a witch. It was all I knew. Being human and then forced into the supernatural world on the whim of another would probably be pretty terrifying. Her comment about being born a vampire surprised me. I didn't know they *could* be born.

"I thank you for your offer, and I accept."

She brought her wrist to her mouth and pierced the flesh with her fangs. "Quickly, before it closes."

She brought her wrist to my lips, careful not to spill any blood on me, and pressed it to my lips.

Colors danced in front of my eyes the moment the first drop hit my tongue. I could smell sounds, hear the feel of her skin against my lips, and feel the scents swirling around us with my flesh as my senses became a jumbled miasma of experiences. I pulled the blood from the wound with my mouth as it it flowed into me and became part of me.

"Not too much, when you feel better, stop."

When the last dregs of weakness left me, I let go of her and fell back to the bed, afraid to move.

"I would have done that sooner, but I did not want to without your consent. That, and I doubt all of your coven would have approved."

"Thank you, Yuki."

"How do you feel?"

"Better, but afraid to move for different reasons." The blood had spread and was leaving me with warm tingling sensations *everywhere*. I remembered how it felt when Yvette had fed from me, I guess that feeling worked both ways. I laughed and rubbed my tummy. Feeding from Yuki hadn't been the sheer jolt of pleasure like being fed from, but it did feel great. Like the after moments of great sex. "Woah."

"Yes. Feeding has many pleasures…"

I nodded and smiled lazily at her.

"Are you ready to try to stand again?"

I nodded, lifting myself from my bed and sitting up. "Wow. That's a *lot* better."

"Good. Your wound looks much better, too. The green hue is gone, and the scars faded. You do have two white lines but if you weren't looking for them, they wouldn't be noticeable."

She was looking at my neck as she spoke and reached out, tracing her finger down the scar. It sent a shiver down my spine.

"Sorry," she mumbled and pulled away, offering me a hand to help me stand.

She is so beautiful.

I gasped.

Did I offend her? I must apologize. Why is she staring at me?

The thoughts weren't mine. I knew it from the first moment they raced through my head. Each one of them had echoed in my brain in Yuki's voice.

"I can hear you."

"The blood might have amplified your senses. You might be able to see and hear better for a short time."

"That's not what I meant."

What is she saying?

"I'm saying I can *hear* your thoughts…"

"I'm sure it is just your imagination." *Maybe I gave her too much and it is affecting her, causing hallucinations. I remember having long conversations with my deceased grandmother the first time.*

"Thank you. I think you're pretty, too. You didn't offend me, so you have nothing to apologize for. I was staring because I could hear you. I think the smallest amount of your blood would have had the same effect, and speaking to the deceased is a gift, a chance to say goodbye."

No. She can't…

"Yes. Yes, I can. What is going on?"

Great green globs of greasy grimy gopher guts…

"Little bloody birdy butts, mutilated monkey meat," I finished the child's song in her head. She gasped and slid back away from me. "Yuki, what happened?"

"I do not know, but this is not good."

"Why? Because I can hear your thoughts?"

"Think something at me. Can I hear you?"

Yuki! What the hell did you do to me?

"Are you thinking anything?"

"Yes. I'm screaming your name in my head."

"Well, your thoughts are safe apparently." *She has my blood flowing through her veins, but she should not be able to hear me. I need to guard my thoughts.*

"Well, I can hear you. Every word. And try guarding your thoughts. See if that helps. Try to keep me out."

I hope this works. Please don't hear me, there is a wall between us. A wall you can not breach. I am a fortress.

"Apparently a fortress of glass."

Shit fuck.

"Language."

She blushed.

"I'm teasing."

This can not be possible. This is horrible.

"Why? Maybe it will wear off once your blood leaves my system. It's probably just a temporary thing."

I hope so. I have a bad feeling.

"It's okay, Yuki. Want me to call Mr. Abernathy and ask him?"

The fear in her eyes was all the answer I needed. I didn't need to hear her thoughts.

"Okay, I won't!"

Nobody can find out about this. "I will see if I can find out what went wrong. You are a witch. I did not think this would be a possibility. I've given blood to a human before, but I have now trodden into unfamiliar territory. Forgive me." She bowed from her waist.

"Stand up straight, Yuki. You were only trying to help. Are you okay?"

She had stopped bowing and was standing rigidly in front of me with a horrified look on her face.

Release me, please!

"Relax! What the hell is going on?"

As soon as I told her to relax, she let out the breath she had sucked in and stood there limply. "We are in so much trouble."

"What? Why? What just happened?" Fear started to creep into *my* stomach.

"Tell me to do something."

"Calm down."

I could see the worry and fear fade from her face, and she began breathing normally.

"Now explain to me in detail what just happened to you."

"I had been bowing, begging your forgiveness. You spoke and told me to stand up straight. When the words left your mouth, it felt like they settled in my flesh. Every muscle in my back forced me to stand rigidly upright at attention. I lost complete control of myself for a moment. I don't think I've been that afraid in a very long time. Even now when you told me to explain in detail, I must convey every nuance of what transpired as well as my emotional state during the events in question."

She looked to me to see if that was enough.

This is as bad, or worse, than I feared. Not only can I hear her every thought, she is being forced to obey me, I thought to myself. *She's almost acting like a familiar… Oh no!*

"Oh, shit," I said aloud.

She knows what has happened. Hopefully she knows how to fix this.

"Yeah. I do know. But there's good news and bad news."

Yuki's face fell.

"The good news is it's not as bad as you think. You've met my Mother's feline familiar, Ichibod?"

"No? Your mother and I have only crossed paths twice. She was alone both times."

"Well…how do I put this…we can *bind* certain creatures to us, to be our eyes and ears. They protect us and…are devoted to us."

"We have similar relationships with wolves and sometimes bats– Wait. Out of curiosity, how do you bind these creatures to you?"

She was catching on. "We um…it's a complicated magic ritual, often taking hours or sometimes days if the creature is strong. And it involves imbibing a minuscule amount of their blood to complete, freely given…"

Blood. Freely given. She drank my…

I heard her thoughts and saw the light flicker on in the attic. I desperately tried to drown out the string of mental expletives that followed, as well as the swelling of anger flowing from her. I let her carry on, wincing at every word and nodding. When she was finished, she stood there in front of me, panting.

234

"What's the good news? Please tell me you can break this."

I sighed. She wasn't going to like this. "That *was* the good news. The bad news is it cannot be undone. Where do you think the words, 'Til death do us part,' came from?"

Her face fell and bloody tears began falling from her cheeks onto the pretty area rug I had picked up at a reasonable price.

No.

"Yes. I'm sorry, Yuki." I toed the rug beneath my foot, not wanting to see the look in her eyes.

"Answer me truthfully, please. You owe me that much. Did you know this could happen? Did you plan this?"

"Absolutely not." I sat back down on the bed. "I wasn't kidding when I said it was a complicated ritual. Most of our magic is just words, intent, and magic. Some require complex diagrams that require long periods of time to perfect. One mishap cannot only cause the spell to not work, in can cause it to work incorrectly or even backfire. We're talking insane amounts of magical damage. There is also a reason we can only bind small animals or smaller magical creatures to us. The larger the creature's will, the greater the chance it won't work."

"So how the hell did you bind me then?"

"I have no idea. I'm sorry, I've never heard of this happening before. Ever."

Lucky me.

I sighed and put my head in my hands.

If the others find out about this… If Lord Abernathy *finds out… I may as well move to Alaska. They might not be able to find me there. To be controlled by a witch would not be taken lightly.*

"Then we won't tell them. You carry on as if nothing is different. I'll do the same. The coven, my mother, everyone will be left in the dark. And you can rest easy, I will *never* control you."

Is she serious? She told me to relax and I almost took a nap.

"I will never *purposely* control you and I will make a conscious effort to be careful what I say around you."

"Dot. Don't take this the wrong way, but I need to stay far away from you. My life as a vampire is on the line–"

She must have noticed the look on my face.

"What, now?" She sighed and sat on the bed away from me, staring at me intently.

"You saw my face?"

"No. I could feel your fear. I might not be able to hear your thoughts, but I can feel your emotions, apparently."

"The...*creatures*–no, I'm not calling you a creature– that become our familiars often gain power and abilities from the binding."

"So, you're saying this could happen to me?"

"Yes. Be careful."

"What *aren't* you telling me."

"That our familiars are driven to be by us. Any length of time away and they start to...suffer."

Fuck me.

"That's one thing I will never do. You don't have to worry about that."

She blinked and then figured out what she'd said, blushing furiously.

I scooted closer to her and tentatively reached over and stroked her hair. "I'm really sorry. I didn't mean for this to happen."

"Why does your hand feel so good right now?"

She was looking up, unable to see my hand. I pulled it away. "Sorry. It's why witches pet their familiars. It's a mingling of power and actually feels comforting to us, too."

"That could get awkward. But, do it again."

I laughed and stroked her hair again, sighing. "I'm sorry, Yuki."

"I know you are. You didn't do it on purpose. All I ask is that you help me keep it from the others."

Epilogue

I stood up and looked down the length of the festive tablecloth covered dining tables. I'd had to buy another one to accommodate the eleven witches in our coven, plus Herb and Marge. I'd found out they were planning on dining alone at home. They'd gotten up and prepared a hundred turkey dinners, loaded them in their delivery van, and distributed them to a list of people who needed them. I had promised them help at Christmas, I just don't think they understood what that meant. I almost cackled gleefully thinking about it, as I'd already started making preparations. Well, Jason had, but they were my ideas.

I smiled at Alista. She had already joined our coven and would be flying back to Ashville with Bill and I in the morning. She and her brother would be closing down the bakery, the sale already going through. We'd found them a nice location to set up on Main Street, right by the bookstore. We were actually going to sell their treats *in* the bookstore, too. Hopefully driving business to them by putting a nice display case in the café. Alista was changing before my eyes. Gone was the shy wallflower, leaving a confident, talented witch in her place. She giggled when Dennis whispered something in her ear.

Everybody stopped whispering as they noticed me standing and holding my glass of wine up. "To the Coven of the First Moon, the Lady has blessed us, bringing us together for this feast. I am *so* thankful that she brought me to you and brought all of you into my life. And also, to our first human friends who know what we are and still came tonight anyway." I winked at Herb and Marge. They laughed and pointed at the engraved seat placards sitting in front of them on the table. Fair was far. I had a seat in their restaurant and they had ones in my home. "Blessed be."

I raised my glass to them and took a sip, letting the white wine calm my nerves as I waited for the sun to set. Even asleep, I could feel Yuki's anxiousness to come join the festivities. While she couldn't eat, we discovered something amazing. When around me, she could taste any food I ate, much to her amazed satisfaction.

That alone had softened the blow of the binding. To taste food had almost made her cry. She'd been trying to talk me into taking her into Syracuse one night to a sushi restaurant. I'd reluctantly agreed. The thought of eating raw fish didn't sit well, but I owed her at least that much. I just hope she didn't pick an all you can eat buffet…

I would be seeing Mr. Abernathy while we were in Ashville, too. Candace had come through and gotten me the exact information he and I had been looking for. The Cedar Falls Blood Bank supplied the hospital some quantities of blood, but had been struggling with poor management and a lack of donations. I had little doubt he would purchase it cheaply, and bring new life, for lack of a better word, to it. He planned on supplying blood to surrounding hospitals for a large profit, as well as supplying the needs of our small vampire population.

A population, I'd found, he intended on increasing. Yuki had let the thought slip one night in conversation. Vampires kept flocking to Ashville for safety. His clan had grown too large and Yuki and George were to be the first of a larger group. I didn't mind, as long as all of them kept their fangs to themselves. Yuki wasn't worried at all and I trusted her. She couldn't lie to me.

We tore into the food. I wasn't the greatest cook in the world, but turkey I could do. An addict needs to be able to supply themselves. Everyone else brought the side dishes. Herb made a mean green bean casserole and jellied cranberries with walnuts and orange liqueur. Bill's mashed potatoes were lumpy and had the skins still on them. I could eat them with enough gravy. I smiled at him as I took a bite. Jimmy's sweet potatoes were yummy for sweet potatoes, but at the end of the day they were just that. Sweet potatoes. They ranked right up there with sushi.

Candace, on the other hand, had made tiny stuffed pumpkins. She'd scraped them, stuffed them with chopped nuts, herbs, and veggies, baked them and covered them with a candy like coating. She made four of them since she didn't eat turkey and insisted that I try one. I watched her as she took her spoon, whacked it to crack the candy shell, and pulled the small lid off with a puff of steam.

I did likewise, and the smell was amazing. She smiled as I reached in with my fork and took a bit, making sure to get some of the pumpkin flesh with it. The taste almost made me cry. She had taken every aspect of fall, ground it up into a crunchy fluffiness, and baked it into something that was half-dinner and half-dessert. I finished it off before cutting into my turkey.

She looked *so* happy. After the kidnapping, Bill had paid a visit to the hospital to give them a watered-down version of what had happened. When Candace called to take a couple of weeks off, at my suggestion and almost insistence, they had eagerly told her to take all the time she needed. I was glad they did. I wanted to spend my first holiday in Cedar Falls with my entire new family. Even Dennis, who was supposed to be working, managed to switch shifts.

Once the holiday was over, I wanted a few days away from them…

Since I had gotten munched on and almost died, to call them clingy would have been the understatement of the year. I hadn't had a moment alone since. I understood their fear of losing me, but I wasn't going to the Lady for a long time. I promised them. Even if it killed me. They didn't appreciate my humor.

I winked at Josie sitting next to Candace. She had been a bigger mess for a few days. We had gotten Candace back unhurt, but then she blamed herself for not only letting her get kidnapped, but for my injuries, as well.

I'd broken her out of her funk to tell her I wasn't just fine but had actually gotten something out of it in return. A shiny new familiar with pointy teeth and piercings. Yuki had been a little upset at me telling her but got over it. Josie was not only my best friend, but also a part of who I was. I couldn't keep it from her. She would have been pissed as all hell if she found out on her own.

My doorbell rang in slow motion, sounding distorted to me. I turned my head slowly in the direction of the living room. A sense of unease washed over me. Everyone seated around me turned their attention toward me.

"I'll get it," I said with a horrible sense of déjà vu.

Lady, if you're listening, don't let it be a werewolf, or anything like that, needing help. I can't take it again. Not this soon…

I reached out and unlocked the door, turning the brass knob and pulling it open, peeking around the edge of the door.

The man standing in my door wasn't *overly* tall, a few inches under six-feet. His normally shoulder length wavy brown locks had been pulled into a messy ponytail and was a lot longer than the last time I'd seen him. His soft green eyes squinted in amusement. Delicate lips curled up into a smile as he roughly said, "Surprise!"

His voice touched places it had no business touching as my knees went a little weak. The last time I'd seen him had been decades ago. His mother had grown bored with America and wanted to go back to Dublin to open an apothecary. He was just a few years older than me but had been just as inexperienced the first time I'd given myself to him, or anyone. We'd dated for months before he told me they were leaving.

"Derek? Derek Flynn?"

"In the flesh. Sorry to drop in unannounced, but yer mother said I should surprise ye."

"She did, did she?"

He must have sensed something or saw the look in my eye. "Should I not have?"

"No. Not a fan of surprises and she knows that. You should have told me you were back the moment you got there. Then I would have told you to come see me." I reached out and hugged him, nothing more. He felt as good as he smelled and had filled out nicely in the forty or fifty years it had been since I'd last seen him. "Come in and grab a seat and a plate. Happy Thanksgiving."

"Thank ye, Dorothea. It's good to see ye. I've missed ye."

He walked past me and began greeting my coven as he rounded the corner. I slowly shut the door and turned my eyes upward. "I'm grateful for that, too."

"Who is this?" Jimmy asked me, sounding a little suspicious.

"An old friend," I answered, blushing uncontrollably and unable to meet his eyes.

"I wouldn't call the guy you gave your virginity to an old friend, Dot," Josie answered, being her usual unhelpful self.

I kicked her off my best friend list and replaced her with the glass of wine in front of me.

Bonus Scene!

Enjoy the Lambresco's restaurant scene in Chapter 15 from Chief's point of view!

The Chief of Lambresco's

My eyes glanced nervously at the clock on the fireplace for the twentieth time. I had nothing else to do. Jimmy was taking Dot to the restaurant at exactly seven. I'd gotten off work at five, and in a nervous panic, ran home, showered, and got dressed an hour too early. Sitting in Becca's chair, I sipped at the beer that didn't even remotely taste good. Kind of funny how your nerves can spoil the flavor of even your favorite things.

I wasn't lying. I'd have been nervous just *taking* Dot on a date. When I'd gotten the call from Jimmy to come watch them have dinner together, I'd been kind of sick to my stomach. But then the pervert said something that got to me. "I'll be eating with her, but Bill...this is *your* date. Trust me."

Trusting him would normally have been my last reaction. Not that he wasn't trustworthy, I'd known the guy for years...but his quirks were a little too quirky. Don't even get me started on his kinks. I'd heard some of the stories from the guys at the fire department. There was just something in his voice when he called. I hoped it wasn't pity, but I decided to give him the benefit of the doubt. Dating Dot…had its own set of difficulties. I didn't need Jimmy making it any harder.

I set the beer down on the table beside Becca's chair and tilted my head back, trying to breathe in anything of her, her scent…or even just a feeling. I would have given my life to hold her once again, but she'd been gone for over two years. I knew she would want me to move on, it was just hard. Picking up her picture, I set it in my lap, letting my finger trace the curve of her face, touching her face always calmed my frayed nerves.

"You'd like her, Becca. I'm sorry you didn't get to meet her. She's everything we need and more. I think we're going to be all right. She's even taking care of your brother."

The tears slid down my cheeks before I knew they were coming. "I *miss* you. Still. Every damn day."

I could almost see the worry in her eyes, and the disappointment. Not from finally moving on, but the close calls I'd had in the past two years. Five times I'd come close to taking my own life just to hold the woman who had been taken from me too soon. Now, the thought of it made me sick. I was a coward, but mostly I thought I was hopeless and lost without her. If she were still alive, she would have kicked my ass.

I still couldn't clean my gun. Once I'd had the taste of gun oil in my mouth, known how close I'd come, just the smell of it made me shake uncontrollably. The guys on the force just thought I didn't like guns, that I was afraid to draw. That I gave the bad guys too many chances. The truth was, there was always the nagging doubt that I might turn it around on myself in a moment of weakness. If I could do my job without one…I would.

Then Dot walked into my life. Sure, she drove me fucking nuts, but any woman worth spending time with shouldn't be perfect. They should be perfect for you. And she was. In spades. She drove me crazy, we fought, she drank too much, and she was ten times sexier than any woman should be, but fuck if I wasn't having the time of my life. Sometimes I wanted her to piss me off just to feel alive again. I loved her, I needed her, I was addicted to her, and I couldn't live with out her. But I felt horrible because part of my heart had gone to the grave with my wife. It was the half that wanted a house, love, a family...

Dot was Dot. She was mine, I was hers, but I'd never be the only man in her life. I couldn't be. I wasn't whole. She needed way more than I could ever give her alone, and I was good with that. For the first time in a long time, as I sat there in Becca's chair, I smiled instead of cried.

I could almost feel Becca's sweet kiss on my forehead.

I checked the time once more. If I drove slowly, I'd get there on time. Not too early, not too late. Making sure I had my keys, I headed for Lambresco's.

The great thing about driving a police car was watching the shady people scramble as I drove past. *Way to look innocent, asshole.* The bad thing is having to wave and smile at the not so shady people as they go out of their way to show you that they're not shady. It was a vicious, never ending cycle.

The clock on the Jeep's radio changed to seven just as I pulled into the parking lot. I lucked out and found a spot not too far from the door, either. My palms were so sweaty my hand slipped on the steering wheel as I turned into the spot. I hoped I didn't soak my shirt as my nerves turned on the faucets of my sweat glands. Nobody wanted a sweaty date, even if they're weren't sitting at the same table as you.

"If it's too much, I can always leave." I cocked an eyebrow at myself in the rearview mirror.

With one last sigh, I opened the door and headed inside, letting my eyes adjust to the dim lighting.

"*Buonasera,* Chief."

I blinked at the older Italian lady who greeted me at the door. She was holding a menu and seemed to be waiting for me. Knowing Jimmy, she probably was. I'd eaten there a few times, and I'd seen her before, but for the life of me, I couldn't remember her name.

"Hey. How you doing?"

"Good! Good to see you again. Follow me, I have your table all ready."

I'm sure you do.

She headed toward the back of the restaurant and as soon as we got to the aisle of booths, I saw her. My heart stopped beating, climbed its way out of my chest, and lodged in my throat. I swallowed, not to force it down, but to take a moment to get used to seeing her beautiful face again. She really was. Sexy. Beautiful. Funny. Oh, my goddess she was funny. When she wasn't driving me insane, or driving me insane with desire, she made my sides hurt from laughing and my face hurt from smiling.

But it was the look on her face that made me feel a thousand times better about agreeing to watching them have dinner. She was more afraid than I was. I could see it on her face in an instant. I felt selfish for worrying. It wasn't me who was stepping way out of her comfort zone, it was her. I smiled at her and nodded at Jimmy sitting next to her as the hostess herded me into my seat, directly across and diagonal from them. It was the best seat in the house with the most beautiful of views.

"May I get you something to drink?"

"I think I'll have wine," I told her. The taste of the beer earlier still felt wrong, somehow.

"Be right back," she said and walked over to their table to take their order, interrupting their discussion. They ordered spaghetti and some chicken dish I'd never heard of and the waitress winked at me as she walked by. I looked up just in time to see Jimmy lean over and take Dot's ear between his lips. She almost shot out of the booth like a rocket. I knew she was on edge, I just hadn't known how much.

Then he whispered something into it. She said something about squid, but looked a little more relaxed. Safer even. Whatever he told her, I saw the tension drain from her as she looked at him adoringly. For the first time in my life, I wanted to be Jimmy. Just to have her look at me like that.

I gazed at the menu, not really knowing what to order, and having trouble keeping my eyes on the menu anyway. Dot rubbed her face on Jimmy's shoulder and took a sip of her wine as he absentmindedly rubbed her leg. How he could be touching her and focusing on anything else was beyond me. She felt like fire, tasted like wine, and smelled like sunshine.

They conversed and I tried not to look like I was straining to hear every word, but then I was distracted when the hand he had been running over her leg slid up her dress and exposed her to me. Thankfully I hadn't been holding my glass, or I would have spilled everywhere.

I couldn't see her most intimate of areas because her legs were closed, but just seeing her there, in a dress up to her waist, was enough to make me harden. I reached down and adjusted my pants, giving myself a little room to grow.

I swear to the goddess she wasn't wearing anything under her dress. I don't think my eyes left her while they talked, giggled, and did date type things that had nothing to do with me. For the moment, she was his. They were the show and I was just the audience. I wasn't jealous of him, but I would have traded places with him in an instant. Time spent with Dot was time worth living. I found myself smiling at them. They really were a cute couple and you could tell Jimmy was just as infatuated with her as I was. He hung on her every word.

Suddenly she flipped her dress down and the waitress brought them their soup and salad and came by to take my order. I mumbled the first thing I remembered from the menu and she was off. I could have ordered cow testicles drowned in Ragu for all I knew or cared. Hopefully I managed to pick something edible. But it really didn't matter. Especially when Jimmy set his spoon down and slid his hand over her leg. Then the ambidextrous son of a bitch started eating with his left hand and kept playing with his right. I was in awe. I would have flung soup on my face and everybody else three booths back.

His finger slipped between her thighs and I nearly knocked over my wine. I could tell he was playing with her tuft of hair and she let him, without saying a word. Then he parted her legs. Not just a little, he pulled her leg over his and her other opened on its own. I couldn't help myself. I no longer needed dinner, I was feasting on her with my eyes. It was one of the most glorious sights I'd ever seen.

I jumped when the waitress set my salad down in front of me. I wanted to cry. Dot had shut her legs, but as soon as the waitress delivered the food and left, she parted them again, glancing at me nervously as she did. It wasn't Jimmy putting on a show for me, it was Dot. She was enjoying it almost as much as me. I kept looking up at her eyes as she ate, making eye contact with her, trying to show her with my eyes how beautiful she was, and then back down to her exposed pussy. I wanted to throw my salad on the floor and crawl over to her and taste her. My cock had gone from stiff to rigid and it was straining against my pants. Of course, Jimmy pointed it out to her, they were both staring under my table for a change.

Let them. At least I'm covered. I can see all *of her.*

Dot suddenly slammed her legs together and sat up a little straighter. The waitress swished past me and delivered their food. She picked up some of their dirty dishes and winked as she passed me again. I chuckled nervously and stopped cold as Dot opened her legs again. She even hiked her dress up a little. I could see the soft flesh just above her hair. It was unfair to me that her pubic hair was just as fiery as the hair on her head. It was one of the most erotic things I'd ever seen. I wanted to run my fingers through it.

Who am I kidding? I want to rub my face against it.

They started eating and Dot just sat there exposing herself to me as she daintily ate little slivers of her food. Jimmy continued eating with his left hand and slid his other hand down over her mound, cutting off my view, but giving me another show. He caressed her lips, sliding around and through them. I could almost hear her squish as he pressed his fingers together. She was wet enough for me to see it and knowing how turned on she was made it even hotter. He slowly began to rub her, massaging that wetness into her as he ate and pretended nothing was going on.

I couldn't stop myself. Even if I wanted to. My hand had a mind of its own and it slipped under the table and over my cock. It had been years since anyone had watched me masturbate, and there I was, doing it in the middle of the restaurant, Dot wasn't even trying to pretend she wasn't watching. Some Chief of Police I was. Exposing myself was a misdemeanor. Stroking my cock in a restaurant was right on the verge of a felony...

Jimmy said something to her, and she kissed him as he rubbed her pussy. A moment later, her eyes were back on me as her breathing became a series of ragged gasps. Jimmy slipped a finger inside her and she came. I almost spurted in my pants watching her try to not scream someone's name as her body tightened and convulsed while she held a forkful of food in her hand.

He said something again, and she straightened, eating the bite she'd been holding while he continued to gently caress her sodden lips.

Dot had closed her eyes and the waitress set a plate of food down in front of me. I'd ordered some sort of pasta, apparently. Dot was lost in pleasure and I wanted to signal her. I just prayed the waitress hadn't noticed.

"She is beautiful, no?"

So much for my prayers. "Absolutely gorgeous."

"Mister Jimmy told me to tell you to wait for dessert..." She chuckled and left me sitting there, raging hardon still in my hand. Thank the goddess I hadn't pulled it out of my pants.

Dot opened her eyes just as the waitress left again. I saw the panic when she'd realized what happened, but Jimmy said something to her, and she shrugged. Calmed for now.

She'd finished her meal and pushed her plate away. I was absentmindedly chewing mine, still watching. Dot closed her legs when the waitress came back with another round of drinks and a simple plate of strawberries.

Oh, fuck. He's gonna go nine-and-a-half weeks on her.

Dot knew. She said something to him and then spread her legs as the waitress left us alone, hopefully for the last time. Dot reached down, finished off her one glass of wine, and then downed the second without spilling a drop. I chuckled. She knew she needed liquid courage.

I was half-hoping to watch him run the strawberries through her wetness, but he teased her mouth with them. When she tried to bite one, he would pull it away. Finally, he let her taste their sweetness as he reached down with his free hand and let his fingers slide through her. She was

252

being pleasured from both ends at once and it was driving her nuts.

I watched, mesmerized, as they played their game with the strawberries. She was close to coming again. His fingers glided over her soft wet flesh and she quivered with every stroke and every bite, the taste of the strawberries and the pleasure from her pussy. She'd never be able to think about strawberries again without feeling the tingle, which is what I was sure Jimmy had planned from the start.

Finally, they were down to one and I knew dessert was coming to an end. He reached out and plucked it from the plate, slipping it under the table instead of bringing it to her mouth. I watched in rapt fascination as the tip glided through her wet folds. He set it on the plate, leaned over and whispered something to her.

She stood and quivered as she did, almost falling over. She closed the distance between us and set the plate down in front of me. "Dessert," she managed to say, and slowly walked back to her table and sat down next to Jimmy, her face buried in her hands.

I frantically grabbed the strawberry, wanting to stuff it in my mouth. Her sweet smell touched my nose before the scent of the strawberry, and I didn't know which was sweeter. Closing my eyes, I took a bite with one hand as I stroked myself.

Jimmy said something to Dot and she spread her legs as far as she could, going so far as to put one of them up on the seat beside her. I stopped chewing as Jimmy reached down and pulled her dress up around her stomach. I wanted to lick every inch of her that had become exposed. He made no pretense of teasing her or touching her. He went for the kill. As his hand glided over her open pussy, he plunged his middle finger inside and finger fucked her to an orgasm in the middle of the room. Her eyes met mine as she thrashed until he slid a hand over her mouth to muffle her screams as she came.

I was at my peak. Letting go of my cock before I made a mess in my pants, I rushed to the men's room. I had my cock out before my ass touched the sink, not even bothering to hide what I was doing if someone walked in. I'd never been so desperate to come in my life.

And then Dot walked through the door.

She avoided eye contact, only looking at my cock with a hungry look on her face. This was part of the game. I was the audience, and she was the show. Without a word, she knelt in front of me and slowly sucked me into her mouth. Warm, wet, inviting. It was heaven and it was hell. The pleasure was intense, but I wanted to throw her up on the sink and slide myself inside the pussy I'd been staring at hungrily for the last hour.

Next time.

She worked me in her mouth with gliding motions of her hand. I felt my tip rubbing against the back of her throat as she tried to take as much of me as she could into her mouth and felt the familiar tingle and throbbing in my balls. I was going to erupt soon. I groaned from deep in my chest and let it out, hopefully not too loudly, as the first spasm overtook me. I tapped her to give her fair warning, but she knew. She could feel me throbbing as it traveled up my shaft and the first shot emptied in her mouth.

She groaned as I erupted, and I fought not to cry out. I was panting, sweaty, exhausted, and still hard as she stood, tucked me back into my pants, and left me alone in the men's room, wondering what the hell had just happened and how I was still standing.

Author's Note

Reviews are important for new authors and I greatly appreciate everyone who takes a moment to leave one, even a line or two! Thank you so much for reading my reverse harem series! I'm writing away and more books will be out soon!

Follow me on Amazon to be sent updates on my new releases!

Come join my Readers Group on Facebook for news, fun, games, teasers for upcoming books, and naughty shenanigans! 18+ recommended.

Coven of the First Moon

About the Author

A late comer to the writing game, Jacquelyn had always been a fan of romance novels and lately become addicted to the reverse harem category. I mean seriously, who wouldn't? Sitting alone one night she flipped open her laptop and said, "I'm going to give this a whirl." And thus, the Lovin' the Coven series was given life. She has designs on other series as well, but only time shall tell.

As for her, she is five-foot-something, with graying hair, wicked eyes, an eager smile, and an annoying laugh. She lives at home with her dog, a cat, and that is about all she is comfortable sharing.

Other Works

Lovin' the Coven Series
(Reverse Harem- 7 book series)

First Moon
Second Blood
Third Charm
Fourth Rite
Fifth Essence
Sixth Sense
Seventh Seal

The Fox and the Hounds
(Reverse Harem – trilogy)

A Tail of Woah
A Tail of Two Kitties
The Tell Tail Heart